BEYOND
THE
POSEIDON
ADVENTURE

Books by PAUL GALLICO

Novels

ADVENTURES OF HIRAM HOLLIDAY
THE SECRET FRONT   THE SNOW GOOSE
THE LONELY   THE ABANDONED
TRIAL BY TERROR   THE SMALL MIRACLE
THE FOOLISH IMMORTALS   SNOWFLAKE
LOVE OF SEVEN DOLLS   THOMASINA
MRS. 'ARRIS GOES TO PARIS
LUDMILA   TOO MANY GHOSTS
MRS. 'ARRIS GOES TO NEW YORK   SCRUFFY
CORONATION   LOVE, LET ME NOT HUNGER
THE HAND OF MARY CONSTABLE
MRS. 'ARRIS GOES TO PARLIAMENT
THE MAN WHO WAS MAGIC
THE POSEIDON ADVENTURE
THE ZOO GANG   MATILDA
THE BOY WHO INVENTED THE BUBBLE GUN
MRS. 'ARRIS GOES TO MOSCOW
MIRACLE IN THE WILDERNESS
BEYOND THE POSEIDON ADVENTURE

General

FAREWELL TO SPORTS
GOLF IS A FRIENDLY GAME
LOU GEHRIG, PRIDE OF THE "YANKEES"
CONFESSIONS OF A STORY WRITER
THE HURRICANE STORY   THE SILENT MIAOW
FURTHER CONFESSIONS OF A STORY WRITER
THE GOLDEN PEOPLE
THE STORY OF "SILENT NIGHT"
THE REVEALING EYE, PERSONALITIES OF THE 1920'S
HONORABLE CAT   THE STEADFAST MAN

For Children

THE DAY THE GUINEA-PIG TALKED
THE DAY JEAN-PIERRE WAS PIGNAPPED
THE DAY JEAN-PIERRE WENT ROUND THE WORLD
MANXMOUSE

BEYOND THE POSEIDON ADVENTURE

BY
PAUL GALLICO

DELACORTE PRESS/NEW YORK

Published by
Delacorte Press
1 Dag Hammarskjold Plaza
New York, N.Y. 10017

Manufactured in the United States of America

Second Printing—1978

Library of Congress Cataloging in Publication Data
Gallico, Paul, 1897–1976
    Beyond the Poseidon adventure.
    I. Title.
PZ3.G13586Be [PS3513.A413] 813'.5'2 77–26905
ISBN 0-440-00453-5

to
IRWIN ALLEN

CONTENTS

FOREWORD

Beyond the Poseidon Adventure is a book brought about wholly by modern times. It is a sequel, not to the original novel, but to the film made from that novel.

The original novel, *The Poseidon Adventure*, was first published in 1969, then bought by producer Irwin Allen and made into a motion picture by him at Twentieth Century-Fox. It appeared in 1972 as the first of the highly successful series of catastrophe movies that followed it.

Every writer knows that when his work is produced as a motion picture the adaptation will impose changes and *The Poseidon Adventure* was no exception. Of necessity characters were dropped, others added, characterizations altered and, in some cases, the plot altered also. But by and large the film reflected the spirit and the plan of the novel.

There is no help for changes made in the transference of the book to the screen. Every sensible producer and writer knows this. Nevertheless the producer still wants his picture to follow the book as closely as possible, particularly when the latter is a bestseller and the former a smash hit.

This last has evoked in Irwin Allen, producer of the film, a desire to make a sequel to the first film.

This is where both producer and writer find themselves in these days when hit movies are followed by sequels using the same characters and sequel novels flower at the same time.

Ever since the rise of the paperback the film has needed the novel, the novel the film. Each aids in the campaigns of publicity and promotion. In the sequel the novel and the film are projected to arrive simultaneously if possible. The problems connected with this in the case of *The Poseidon Adventure* and *Beyond the Poseidon Adventure* were unique. For in the original novel the gallant *Poseidon*, to the sound of the sirens of the surrounding rescue craft, plunges beneath the waves forever and the characters disperse in accordance with the plan of the author.

In the film the *Poseidon* does not sink and we are left with the final scene of the after portion of the upturned hulk with the giant propellers showing, and the surviving characters, Mike Rogo, Manny Rosen, James Martin, Nonnie, and Susan and her younger brother, Robin, being airlifted off from the hull by a French naval helicopter and flying away.

How fortunate! For had not Irwin Allen decided

upon this ending to the picture and with the *Poseidon* at the bottom of the sea no sequel would have been possible.

The novel herewith produced, *Beyond the Poseidon Adventure*, takes the surviving characters as delineated in the motion picture and carries on with some of them as they were, looked, and behaved in the film, the action taking place both inside and outside the partly submerged hulk of the *Poseidon* but with the addition of a whole new starring cast.

The filmmaker must follow his knowledge of how to entertain the viewing public, the novelist must follow his bent on how to intrigue and satisfy his reading public. Thus, it is almost certain that, just as in the first case, the film *Beyond the Poseidon Adventure* will make changes from the novel to the detriment, one hopes, of neither. In some cases the two will go their own ways in accordance with the necessities of their creators.

The main thing to remember is that this book is a sequel to the film and everything that was in that film. If you enjoyed that picture as millions seem to have done I hope perhaps you will be intrigued by, and find entertainment in, what happened to some of these people afterwards.

P.W.G.
Monaco, June 1976

BACK TO THE POSEIDON

1

The thick blanket settled warm and heavy on his shoulders and the hot coffee burned sweetly in his mouth. Rogo waited for the sense of relief to wipe away the fear and tension. It didn't.

"You are the lucky man, *monsieur*."

The precise voice of the French warrant officer jerked him out of his bitter thoughts.

"Huh?" Rogo grunted.

The helicopter was swinging in a great angled sweep of the sky and the officer pointed through the window to the wreckage of the S.S. *Poseidon* below. "I said you are the lucky man," he repeated. "Sixteen hundred dead and only six saved. We must thank God, I think."

Rogo finished the rest of the coffee in the plastic cup. "You thank Him, pal," he said. "He ain't done me no favors."

The Frenchman raised incredulous eyebrows and backed onto his seat on the port side of the machine, where Manny and Martin offered more agreeable company. "We certainly do thank God, sir," Martin chirruped. "Mr. Rogo's rather tired." He raised his face to Rogo and called out, "But we did it okay, Mr. Rogo, didn't we? We got out after all."

Rogo decided to ignore the little shopkeeper. There were other, more serious things that occupied him. He pressed his pugnacious face against the cold of the window and looked down.

The ship lay on the sparkling waters of the Mediterranean like a surfacing whale. The tidal wave that had tossed it over so easily had left it upside down and two-thirds submerged. He could see the huge propellers jutting upwards like ears, and the square cut the French rescue team made in the propeller-shaft housing to release them.

It was impossible to imagine that about eight hours earlier it had been packed with carefree merrymakers celebrating New Year's Eve. Now they were all dead. His wife Linda. Manny Rosen's wife, Belle, and Scott, the fiery minister who had led them to safety. All dead. In some ways, he thought, it would be better if he were down there with them.

For eight hours they had struggled to fight their way through a nightmare of wreckage and bodies and roaring water, and in that topsy-turvy hell it had been hard to count on a normal world outside. Now he was safe in the warmth of the helicopter with a glittering sun overhead, and he wished himself still inside the *Poseidon*.

The warrant officer was checking the names of the survivors on a clipboard. "Let us see if I have the details correct," he said. "Susan and Robin Shelby. They will be the two children who are asleep in the back, yes?" His pencil indicated the rear of the machine where they had been bedded down.

The self-appointed spokesman, James Martin, agreed. "And the girl with them, she's called Nonnie Parry. From Lancaster, Pennsylvania."

He went on brightly as the officer continued to check the names against a list. "I'm James Martin, from Anaheim, California, and this is Mr. Emmanuel Rosen from New York."

The officer murmured his thanks and ticked off more names. "And that," whispered Martin, "is Detective Lieutenant Mike Rogo—he's from New York too. He's quite famous really. He once broke up a prison riot."

The Frenchman shot Rogo a look that suggested he would not be impressed if he had been the first man on the moon. Martin insisted as loudly as he dare. "He did. It was in all the papers."

It was not quiet enough. "Can it," Rogo's growl shrank the little red-haired man back into his seat.

"I was only . . ."

Rogo mimicked his squeaky voice with cruel accuracy. "I was only trying to help, Mr. Rogo." Then he reverted to his own rasping register. "Well, don't."

He turned from his shocked audience and squinted through the window again. All around the steel hull of the *Poseidon* lay the flotsam and jetsam of a shipwreck, the smashed relics of life aboard a cruise liner that were no longer entirely recognizable. He could pick out some things: items of clothing, an empty lifejacket, crates, and, incongruously, a grand piano.

Suddenly Manny Rosen burst into sobs and dropped his weeping face into his hands. "Belle, my Belle, I shouldn't have left you down there."

The Frenchman was astonished by the tenderness of Rogo's response. "Don't take it so bad, Manny. She was a great lady. She saved us all. That's what she wanted to do."

The helicopter was circling again back over the scene. Rogo nodded towards the short staircase that led to the bubble which housed the pilot, copilot, and radio operator. He asked the warrant officer, "Why don't we get the hell outta here?"

The Frenchman ignored his tone. "We must survey the scene to make a full report, sir," he replied. "They will want to know which other ships are in the area and if and when the *Poseidon* is likely to sink. Then we shall take you back to base, and you will be flown to Athens."

Then, thought Rogo, back to New York. And the questions. Why had he left? Why had he not stayed with the job? What had happened to the shipment? For Chrissakes, he groaned inwardly, all those goddamn questions. Then he remembered O'Hagan and that made it worse. Every mill, every office, every classroom has its funny man. O'Hagan was going to love this one. Rogo could imagine it all too easily. "Fell down on the job, huh, Rogo? Quit. Walked out. Must have a yellow streak buried under that fat gut,

Rogo." He gripped his massive fists as he thought about it.

The helicopter continued to circle and climb, and Rogo half-heard Martin's babbling as he told the officer of their terrifying ascent through the bowels of the ship. "Well, it was the Reverend Scott who took charge. He was the minister, you know, a preacher. What a wonderful man! It was his idea to make for the stern. He said it was the best chance of rescue. He tried to tell the others but they wouldn't listen . . ."

Rogo muttered a few weary obscenities to himself. Martin made it sound like an adventure trip. He didn't know, none of them knew, of the weight of shame and responsibility that the policeman would have to bear.

". . . but I guess Scott went kind of funny at the end and he threw himself into a blazing pool. He said something about sacrificing his life for ours. He was very religious." He glanced nervously at Rogo and lowered his voice. "That was when Mr. Rogo's wife died. She fell. And Mrs. Rosen was a real hero. She dived under the water to find a way out for us."

If Manny heard him, he said nothing. His head was still buried in his hands as he sobbed softly.

The blanket fell from Rogo's shoulders as he pressed once more against the window. The sea was no longer empty. To the south there was a white pleasure yacht with a single yellow funnel about ten miles from the *Poseidon*. On the horizon to the north, a blob of black smoke signifying another advancing vessel. And much nearer, almost directly below them, what looked like a scruffy working boat. All were heading for the *Poseidon*.

"Hey you!" Rogo ordered. The Frenchman looked

up with strained courtesy. Rogo went on, "What the hell's going on down there?"

The officer lifted his marine glasses and inspected the scene. He swung them from one vessel to another. "Salvage," he said. "It is customary."

"Customary!" Rogo made the word sound like the eighth deadly sin. "Whaddya mean, for Chrissakes? That tub's got nothing to do with those guys."

The officer lowered the glasses and explained with elaborate patience. "The nearest one looks like a coaster. He will be trying to be the first to get a line on board so he can claim salvage rights. The one furthest away is, I think, the *Komarevo*. She is what you might call a professional scavenger of the seas. Amongst other things. The yacht, I imagine, is doing a little macabre sight-seeing."

Rogo scowled at the yacht. "Rich kids rubbernecking. Don't I just know the type." Then he was questioning the officer across the aisle again and he seemed deeply perturbed. "Why ain't she sunk yet? Jesus, we thought she'd go down any lousy minute."

"Air," the officer replied succinctly. "Air pockets. There must have been many trapped in the forward and aft, now there must be one huge air bubble holding her up. Most of her engines and boilers will have fallen out. You saw them, perhaps?"

Rogo did not answer. "Yeah, but how long can she stay up?"

The officer looked out of the window again; the ships below were now little more than toys. He shrugged. "Five minutes, five hours, five days, five weeks. Remember, she is one-third above the water. There was an iron ore ship, the *Yacob Verolm*, forty thousand tons. She was capsized in a storm, the crew escaped, most of her cargo and engines fell out. She floated, keel up, for forty days."

The policeman slumped back in his seat as though shot. His eyes were open and staring. He did not appear to hear the officer's final comment. "In the end they had to shoot her down."

In a hoarse whisper, Rogo asked, "What happens if it doesn't sink?"

The young Frenchman was frowning. He could not understand Rogo's obvious concern. "Well," he said, "they will try to tow her into shallow water. Then salvage everything they can. Cargo, machinery, anything of value."

Anything of value. Rogo knew what he must do. In his mad dash to escape death, and what had seemed the certainty that the ship was sinking, he had lost sight of his mission. He had forgotten he was a working cop. Now the cargo could be recovered and claimed by God knows who. It would be the end for Rogo. He could hear O'Hagan's taunting voice already. His simple sense of duty and primitive pride boiled inside him, but most of all he could hear O'Hagan.

He slipped his hand into his pants pocket. It was still there. The tiny Colt .25 automatic, no bigger than a bunch of keys. He had scoffed when they had issued it to him. A handbag gun, he had said. You couldn't punch holes in paper with it. He wanted his .38 Police Special, but they had insisted: on a security job you needed a lightweight pistol you could carry at all times. He remembered what Linda had said the previous evening when he had put it in his pocket.

"Who we having dinner with, honey—Frankie Costello?" But it was a gun, it had a full clip of six, and that was all that mattered.

He stood up slowly and flicked the neat two-inch barrel at the French officer.

"Okay fella. Tell the driver to turn around. I'm going back."

The tidal wave which eight hours earlier had been launched by an underwater earthquake was almost entirely directional. The huge wall of water which spun the S.S. *Poseidon* over like a leaf tore across the Mediterranean destroying everything in its path. Fishing vessels and millionaires' yachts, motor cruisers and simple weekend boats were obliterated by that rampaging flood. Even when it hit the northern shores of Africa, it pounded angrily at the land.

Although it struck most savagely to the south, the effects were felt in varying degrees all around the Mediterranean. Tall yachts in safe harbors bucked like thoroughbreds in their stalls; halyards chattered in terror to the metal masts. Tax exiles with sea views dashed to their shutters as they heard their blue and kindly waters suddenly ravage the tourist beaches.

In the wardroom of the Dutch freighter *Magt van Leiden*, Captain Klaas van Zeevogel and his sixteen-year-old daughter Coby were sent spinning from their seats and crashed against the wall, wide-eyed with fear.

A few miles away, the young American at the helm of *The Golden Fleece* felt his thirty-foot Bermudan sloop wrenched from beneath him like a rug and turned into matchwood within a minute.

Then that one huge wave was gone. The seas stilled

to an almost unnatural calm under the clear unseeing eye of the moon.

In those moments of high danger, all the practice and training in the world counted for nothing, and you had to fall back on pure instinct. Sharpen your reflexes on dangerous living all you like, but it was instinct that governed split-second action when there was no time for the rational processes of thought.

Before the wave, he had been at peace. The hours he spent in *The Golden Fleece* seemed to be his only time of true contentment. All day he had enjoyed clear skies. His twenty-five-year-old sloop had cut through the water on a broad reach, genoa and main-sails full, at a good six knots. The sun picked out the laundered whiteness of the patches around the batten holes and the bits of peeling varnish, but nothing could conceal the fact that his was a classic boat of beautiful performance and design, the perfect reflection of a man with taste and spirit. And if such a man should not really have his dinghy inflated and skimming behind the stern, well, it was a relaxed sort of day, everything was going well. As it turned out, his laziness in not bringing the dinghy on board and deflating it saved his life.

Then the wave had hit, and in that moment of atavistic instinct, all he could hope was that his body did the right things. It was exactly the same when he boxed at college. He would see the right cross coming over and, almost as a theoretical exercise, wonder if his left arm would rise to block it and his own right swing over. It was true, too, out there in those jungle-strewn hills. The black leaves against the piercing blue of the sky. One patch would be too black, too solid, and he would drop to one knee and feel the shudder of the automatic in his arms, and after he fell there would be another of those faces, brown and meaningless as the face on a coin.

He had been beating to windward under the clear night sky and watching the bow. In this tideless sea, wind and weather came together. He had heard the noise, turned, and caught a glimpse of that white-capped avalanche roaring through the darkness. Quickly he had thrown the tiller to starboard and brought her through the eye of the wind so that she took the wave across the bow. Even as he did, and felt the sloop tossed like a scrap of paper, he knew it was no use. Not even his yacht could weather that one. Then he was flying over the water and dragged in a great gulp of air before he felt himself rolled and tumbled powerlessly in the all-engulfing dark of the wild waters. He struck upwards through the tumult and his lungs strained when it seemed he would never see the sky again. Then, just as inexplicably, it had gone. He paddled on the rapidly calming surface. The dinghy was there, waiting like a well-trained dog.

He was alive. He had a boat under him. But *The Golden Fleece*, his home, his office, and his love, had gone. With it the highly refined radio equipment that was by no means standard on a sloop of that size, the documents entitling him to collect a shipment of oranges, and the Navy .45 automatic hidden in the cabin sole.

The wooden oars squeaked in the plastic rowlocks. It was a long way to Athens. At this rate, he told himself, he might just make it by next New Year's

Eve. In the meantime, any dockside worker who fancied stealing an orange was in for a considerable surprise.

Across the black water, he thought he saw faint lights. He reached for the flare pistol and muttered three cheering words to himself.

"Happy New Year."

The fifteen-hundred-ton workhorse freighter *Magt van Leiden*, out of Amsterdam sailing on a course of north by northwest which would take her to Athens, split the extraordinary mirror surface of the Mediterranean with her chugging, even progress. Only the almost negligible waves from her stubby bow disturbed the reflection of her own lights on that plate-glass calm.

She was a typical small coaster, with the usual central island from which protruded a short, nondescript buff-colored funnel, double derrick arms fore and aft, a forward well giving access to the crew's quarters, and a single deck encompassing the island and the bridge.

Tramp she may have been, but only by name. She was as neat as a liner, her hull painted black, her superstructure the same buff color as her funnel and the housing of the bridge and quarters an immaculate white. At her stern flew the horizontal red, white, and blue tricolor of the Netherlands.

Everything about the *Magt* suggested decency and probity. The same was true of the chunky, powerful man in his mid-fifties who leaned on the railing of the ship and contemplated with concern the unbroken surface of the sea. He was a solid man, physically as well as temperamentally. He was not tall, but his chest and arms had a heavy, serviceable look about them. The head, well set upon a strong neck, was grizzled, and on the back of it was perched a white yachtman's cap. The gold badge embracing intertwined nautical insignia proclaimed him captain.

A small sticking plaster covered the cut on his chin where he had been flung across the cabin.

He lifted his head and seemed to be sniffing to several quarters like a dog orienting himself. "I do not like it, Coby," he offered, eventually. "I do not like it."

"Why not, papa?"

He looked down at his daughter and saw his own far-seeing dark blue eyes. Her blue-black hair, braided and coiled over her ears, enabled her to ape the angle of her father's cap. But instead of the badge of office, she had pinned on a cheap gilt replica of one of her native country's windmills.

"It smells of earthquake weather," he replied.

"Smells? It actually smells?"

He smiled a little. "No, not really a smell. It is a feeling, a sense. That tidal wave that nearly capsized us, it must have been due to some disturbance of the earth. It is the only possible explanation."

"But it's calm now," she said.

"Too calm. It is not often when the earth shakes like that. I know little about earthquakes, but I shall be happier when we reach Athens. In the meantime, goodness knows how many smaller boats must have been capsized. I will keep watch. You go to bed, Coby. It's long past midnight."

"In a moment," she said. They were quiet for a while, listening to the uneven chugging of the old engines. From time to time he turned and examined the unbroken black of sea and sky.

But it was Coby who saw it first. "Look, papa," she cried and pointed. There was a sudden flame, a rocket trail, and a blinding burst of white light. For two minutes, half a square mile of sea was brilliantly illuminated, and they saw quite clearly a small black boat in the middle of the shimmering light.

Urgently Klaas called up to the bridge. "Bear off six points to starboard, Piet. There's a boat. Make for it."

The light died, and in the dark the *Magt* came upon the dinghy a shade too quickly.

"What the hell are you trying to do, save me or swamp me?" The accent was unmistakably American and the tone amazingly nonchalant for a man stranded at sea.

Klaas called to the bridge again. "Reverse a few turns and then shut down." He switched on his lantern and for the first time they saw their shipwrecked mariner. He looked about as frightened as if he had been walking a dog around the park. He was wearing the denim shirt and worn jeans that is the uniform of every harbor bum hanging around the moneyed ports of the Mediterranean. But there was something about him that suggested the unkempt blond hair was a lack of vanity, nothing more. His face was crinkled into a mass of well-practiced laughter lines in the lantern's glare, and they saw skin stretched over high cheekbones and a long, tough jawline.

"My apologies . . ." Klaas shifted the lantern to ease the glare on his face and waited for him to complete the sentence.

"That's better," he said. "Captain Jason."

Klaas was slightly piqued at the rower's dig at his

seamanship. He called down, "If you're looking for the golden fleece, Captain Jason, I am afraid you are going in the wrong direction. It's the other way, to the west, isn't that right, Coby?"

Eagerly she joined in. "Yes, Colchis is on the east coast of Turkey."

The lone figure was bending over tying the oars to the thwarts. "Wrong," he said. "That's where it was until Jason and the Argonauts took it. It ended up in Thessaly."

Then he turned round and rose, balancing on spaced feet. "But I'm the Jason who lost *The Golden Fleece*. My sloop." He waved a hand behind him. "She went down in that wave."

"We nearly did too," said Coby. She could hardly believe it. Even in her girl-woman dreams she had hardly dare imagine finding a handsome stranger in the middle of the sea at night. And here he was, talking easily, without any apparent concern over what had happened. She was fascinated.

The American hooked his thumbs in his jeans pocket and with a nod towards the flag at the stern said, "But if I know my flags, this looks like just the sort of place where a fella could get himself a Bols. Right?"

THE FRIGHTENED MEN

2

The New Year was little more than two hours old when teleprinters in every major city began clattering out the first details of what looked like the greatest disaster in the history of shipping. But the wave of shock and fascinated horror that the news engendered was felt nowhere with the impact it had in two boardrooms thousands of miles and six international time zones apart: in the offices of the Ionian International Shipping and Finance Consortium in Athens and the International Conglomerate and Worldwide Trust Company in New York.

The scenes were almost interchangeable, save for the clocks. The discreetly muted tones of the decor, the heavy gloss of the polished tables, the dull photographs on the walls of paper mills, factories, distilleries, and industrial plants that indicated the reach of their commercial tentacles. Even the principals had the same plump, well-fed look that comes from the seldom disappointed expectation that doors will always open, and wine come at the correct temperature. They were among the most influential men in the world. They were also among the most frightened.

In Athens, Mr. Stephanos Stasiris stood beside a detailed model of the S.S. *Poseidon* which was on a table in the corner. The giant passenger liner was the Consortium's latest acquisition, and it was Stasiris himself who had organized something unique in big ship operations. His ship visited ports in which, unknown to the passengers, substantial shipments of cargo could be transported to the next landing. That caused frowns among those who valued the old liner's unimpeachable reputation for passenger service and quality, but it was a lucrative trade, made more so because the company was not too insistent that the details listed in the manifest should accurately reflect the cargo itself. This pleased the accountants, and that, as Mr. Stasiris liked to say, was what business was all about.

One brief telephone call had brought him from a New Year's Eve party to the top-floor boardroom in the seven-story office building, and he still shivered in his thin dinner jacket from the cool night air. He watched as the others straggled in. Several were shiny-eyed from drinking; one, he noted with displeasure, was quite unsteady on his feet. They all came dressed in the silk and frilled shirts of the celebrations. So did the two specially invited guests to that exceptional board meeting: the hard-eyed, hard-nosed Minister of Defense, Pularnos, and, his chest coruscating with medals and ribbons, General Dravos.

Stasiris took his seat at the head of the table and rested plump jowls on one broad palm. "Gentlemen," he said, "I think you all know what has happened." His voice was steady, but the rustling of the sheet of paper in his hand betrayed his anxiety.

He continued, "We only have the sketchiest of reports so far, but it appears that at midnight the *Poseidon* was capsized by some form of freak wave. If our latest information is correct, she is floating upside down."

The man who had walked so unsteadily through the door furrowed his brow and tried to work out the significance of the statement. He belched. Stasiris gave a slow, tired blink of the eyes. It was an older man on the president's right who put into words the one question that troubled them all. "Are there . . . ahem . . ." he coughed and looked round apprehensively, "I mean, how many survivors? And how long can the ship stay afloat?"

Stasiris nodded, almost in gratitude that someone had mustered sufficient indelicacy to raise the two crucial issues. There were sixteen hundred lives at stake, twelve hundred passengers and four hundred crew. There were also many more subtle issues involved, questions of international power politics, not to mention the future of every man in that room and a good many outside it. Stasiris was responsible for weighing the balance between the two, and there could be no doubt on which side the weight was heavier. He decided to make that plain from the start.

"To enlarge," he said. "We must of course concern

ourselves with the welfare of our passengers and crew, and most particularly must be seen to do so by the rest of the world. But what we are gathered here for, gentlemen, is to consider the consequences if the unusual nature of the *Poseidon*'s cargo is revealed. I feel sure you all understand me." He looked around. Even the unsteady drunk seemed sober now. Each face registered a struggle to contain panic.

Stasiris went right in. "I have taken two steps which I trust will meet with your approval, against the eventuality of the *Poseidon* staying afloat. Our office is issuing a request to any nearby shipping to leave well enough alone, together with an assurance that a full rescue and salvage operation has already been launched. We must hope in this way to keep off all scavengers."

He noted an approving nod from Pularnos. "And have you," the minister asked, "launched this . . . operation?"

"Indeed," Stasiris picked his words carefully. "I have instructed Captain Ilich Bela to proceed to the scene."

"Bela!" It was the man who had belched earlier. Drink had loosened his reactions too much. "Good God, you know what that man is!"

Stasiris snapped back immediately, "Of course I know what he is. We all do. What do you think this is, you fool? We cannot be too careful."

The drunk slumped back and straightened his lolling head. "That's what you get for playing with politicos," he muttered defiantly.

Stasiris glared at him and reverted to more measured tones. "Captain Bela has a reputation for handling difficult work. And I am afraid we must all face the fact that this operation has now become difficult work. So we must use people with appropriate experience and discretion."

There was a long silence. No one appeared to have any further ideas on the subject. Then General Dravos gave an authoritative tug on his moustache and boomed, "Why bother? I will send in six fighter-bombers and shoot the hulk down."

Stasiris threw back his head and laughed. There was no amusement in the sound. "Excellent, General, excellent. Will you also notify all the photographers and television cameramen too so that the whole world may know what we are doing?"

A sunset colored the general's face.

Stasiris went on, "All we can do for the moment is wait. I would suggest you do not leave the building. Food and coffee will be available. And I must thank you, Minister Pularnos, for joining us tonight."

Pularnos raised a fine, lean face and his intelligent eyes pinned Stasiris. "You must know, of course, that in the event of any failure to maintain security in this operation, the government will deny any form of involvement."

The president did not bother to answer for several seconds. Then, speaking softly, he replied, "I know that, Minister. I also know that no one will believe you."

The scene in New York, enacted on the forty-eighth floor of the Conglomerate building, was a little less tousled and rather more clear-headed. It was mid-evening. The men present were also wearing dinner jackets, velvet bow ties, and cummerbunds of celebration, but they had been dragged here before their festivities had begun.

With them were two nonmembers of the Conglomerate: the Secretary of Defense and an admiral.

They listened carefully, with the occasional expostulation of horror, as the president of the company, Arthur Haven, outlined the situation. He concluded, "So you see, all we can do is sit it out."

"Sit it out!" The admiral looked for support from the worried faces around him. "This is national security, almost global security, you're dealing with. Leave it to the military. We can slip a couple of fish into that old scow and no one will ever know."

The Defense Secretary invited Haven's answer with a tilt of the head. Haven, smoothing his palms slowly down the front of his suit, replied evenly, "Admiral, there may be ships close enough to witness it. There are certainly divers who would afterwards testify. That is out of the question."

The Secretary now spoke. "I think you're right, Arthur. We can't sew it up that way. But it has to be sewn up. There's the whole NATO pact at stake here, even the possibility of war. That must be the overriding consideration for us all."

"That's right," Haven was agreeing. "I'm sure we're all aware of that. I've spoken to Stasiris in Athens and he assures me that he is making arrangements for a special salvage expert to handle the whole thing. We've got to hope he can deliver the goods."

The Secretary was about to speak again when Haven hushed him with a raised hand. "And before you say it, yes, I know that the White House will deny it all until they're blue in the face. But if you think for a moment that you can unload this . . ."

He paused, looked at the ceiling, and slipped his hands into his jacket pockets. He looked down again. "Gentlemen, I must ask you all to stay in the building and we'll hope for a break soon. Okay?"

The emphatic masculinity of the wardroom's dark mahogany and brass was relieved by the adaptations that appeared whenever Coby was on board her father's boat. The table acquired a checked cloth and a small bunch of dried grasses in a jar. The coffee, which accompanied Jason's gin, was served in matching cups and saucers instead of the heavy mugs that Klaas was content to use when he was alone at sea.

"You should be in bed, my girl," he said. Coby grimaced behind his back. He looked at his watch. "Good heavens, it's past two o'clock. We have a vacant cabin forward for you, young man."

Jason nodded his thanks, and ran the drink around his mouth before swallowing. He sighed, and father and daughter together scrutinized him. They liked what they saw, but saw quite different things.

Klaas recognized a man who knew his way around boats. He only had to watch him cross the deck to know that. He looked a lethargic figure now, sprawled out lazily in dirty denims, but Klaas had noted the way he had swung himself over the rail and leapt onto the deck of the *Magt*. He was a man of action. He also liked the sense of privacy about him. He asked little, told less, and rolled the conversation along with light, deft touches. He was an easy man.

What Coby saw, and it brought a shine to her eyes, was a figure of glamour. The slim, six-foot frame which angled out to wide shoulders, and the long wicked grin that sliced his face open like a knife. She sensed too a magnetism in the man. His enigmatic reticence, wittily masked in light talk, drew them forward with their questions. When they had told him they were heading for Athens, he had smiled and said simply that would be fine.

"You were going to Athens in a dinghy?" Coby could not resist the question.

"The Argonauts did okay and they didn't even have a flare pistol," he replied.

Klaas laughed. "But one mistral or *vent d'est* and there would have been no Jason as well as no *Golden Fleece.*"

A rueful look twisted his face. "Yeah. *The Golden Fleece.* She was a beauty. She had the lot. Still classed A-1 at Lloyds, you know. And I needed her for my business."

This time Klaas was not going to miss the opportunity to probe a little. "And what is your business, if I might ask?"

"Oh, sort of parcel delivery," he replied, teasing them gently. Then he seemed to realize their hospitality demanded a little more explanation than that. "I was on my way to Athens to meet a boat and pick up a delivery. That's all."

It was not much, but it was obviously all they were going to get. Coby thrilled to the mystery of the man, and tried again.

"What is an American doing so far from home?"

His grin switched off, and he leaned forward across the table. She saw the piercing blue of his eyes. "The

States? Well, these days it's a bit like being in a sick ward. You know the way people in a hospital talk about their illnesses all the time? In the States all they talk about is the sickness of the country. It's a nation that's composed entirely of people examining their own consciences, everywhere, and all the time."

Klaas was interested. He puffed hard on his stubby pipe to revive the fading embers and then asked, "And is that so bad for a country?"

"I dunno." They saw his eyes cool to a slate gray and his face turn to wood. "All I know is it's bad for a guy who doesn't think his conscience will stand up to scrutiny."

The reply was so unexpected and so artlessly frank that it stopped the conversation. Klaas broke it quickly with a deft change of subject. "And what do we call you apart from Captain Jason?"

The long grin was back. "You could try Susie, but I don't promise you anything," he said, and joined in their laughter.

It did not matter to Klaas. He was just a pleasant young man who was taking a lift to Athens with them: it was not the sort of situation that required character references.

Head tilted, Jason was listening. The engines were thudding unevenly. "Sounds like you've got some trouble there, Captain?"

Klaas nodded. "I'm afraid so. This craft was built in 1912. In 1930 my father put in new engines. Now we hold them together with string."

Almost diffidently, Jason asked, "Could I go down and take a look at them sometime?"

Klaas glanced up. "You an engineer?"

Jason answered shortly, "I've done some. You've got a sharp ship here and I might just be able to squeeze a bit more life out of those old rubber bands you've got down there."

The Dutchman puffed with pride. "I am a widower, Jason," he explained. "I have two loves in my life. The dear old *Magt*, and my daughter here. I do my best to look after them."

Jason warned Klaas with a wink and then turned to Coby and said, "Well, you've got a pretty ship all right, but little Coby wins hands down every time." Together the two men laughed at the crimson which flooded her face. "And now, I'd like to take advantage of that spare cabin if I may."

They were all rising when the cabin door flew open. The blast of air cleared the smoke circling Klaas's head. "Yes, Hans?" the captain asked. The wireless operator handed him a sheaf of papers and left.

"What is it, papa?" Coby tried to lean over his arm to read them.

Her father began to shake his head slowly from side to side. "Tragic, oh so tragic. I knew there would be many boats lost in that wave but . . ." He lifted his face. "A luxury liner, the S.S. *Poseidon*, was struck and upturned by it."

Three long, fast strides took Jason round the table and he snatched the papers from his hand. "The *Poseidon*! My God!" His eyes raced along the lines and he did not seem to notice the couple's shock at his brusque reaction. Then he spoke excitedly. "Look, it says it's still afloat. Upside down, but still afloat. Can we get there, Klaas?" He rattled out the words like bullets.

Puzzled, Klaas replied, "Well, I don't know . . . What is your interest in the vessel? Why is it so urgent? I really don't know." He gave Jason a searching, worried look, and the younger man handed back the papers with a muttered apology and spoke more patiently now.

"That's the ship I was going to meet in Athens. There's a very important . . . okay, parcel if you like, on it. I must pick it up. Perhaps there's still a chance if we can get there."

The irritation was evident in Klaas's unfinished response. "Perhaps so, and perhaps your business is very important, but I am due in Athens . . ."

Jason was studying the *Magt*'s captain closely. Suddenly he changed tack. "Of course. But look, there are thousands of people on board that ship. We may be the nearest vessel."

"Yes," the Dutchman said, rereading the messages. "But the owners have also asked all other ships to keep clear."

"A salvage swindle," Jason said promptly. "It's obvious. Are you going to let that stand in the way of saving perhaps hundreds of lives? Come on now, Klaas, you can't leave them all stuck out there in the middle of the goddamn sea. We can be there by eight in the morning."

Klaas checked his watch and nodded. He was thinking. Coby grabbed his hand between both of hers. She pleaded, "Please, papa, think of all those poor . . ."

"Very well." He had made up his mind. "I shall tell Piet to make for the liner at once." He paused and thought again. "I shall have to claim salvage rights if we are the first vessel there, of course. But the main thing is to see if we can help. I suggest we all get a little sleep."

As he opened the door, he looked back and caught the relief on Jason's face. "In the morning, Captain Jason, I shall hope for a fuller explanation. Your amusing mysteries are beginning to trouble me now."

"IT'S A DISAPPOINTING WORLD"

3

At first the French officer had been quite unable to take in the combination of Rogo's bizarre request and the gun in his fist. He gaped.

Then he said, "But, *monsieur*, this is impossible."

"No, it isn't," Rogo replied. "I'm going back on board that tub and you're taking me. Now tell the guys up there." The barrel of the gun indicated the steps leading to the pilot in the bubble.

The Frenchman still could not accept that Rogo was serious. There was a placatory note in his voice as he said, "*Monsieur* Rogo, there is no reason on earth why you should return. It is dangerous. It could sink. And our orders are . . ."

Impatience flared in Rogo's face. He fished his left hand into his trousers and produced his gilt badge. "You take your orders from this now, buddy, so tell those fellas to turn around."

Again the officer spoke reasonably. "Yes, I see the badge, but *monsieur* the lieutenant must understand that this badge has no jurisdiction here. When we reach base, of course, you may put your request to the commandant and perhaps he will agree."

Rogo stepped forward and jammed the slim pistol into the officer's stomach. "Okay, forget the badge. This is my authority from here on out."

For a moment there was complete silence aboard the craft. Every clack of the engine turning the huge rotors sounded louder than ever. The officer looked down at the gun, gave a small shrug and called up the stairs, "Marcel, Eddy, I have a gun pushed into my stomach by a madman who wishes to go back to the ship."

After a pause, a voice came back, "What did he forget—his hat?"

The tremble in the officer's words underlined his sincerity. "There is no joking, I promise you. Please do as he says and return."

A face appeared at the top of the short staircase and looked down. "*Mon Dieu!* He really means it."

Rogo confirmed, "You gotta believe it, pal. Now get moving and don't touch that transmitter."

The pilot had seen enough in that one moment to understand the seriousness of the situation. "If you are determined, *monsieur*, there is little we can do about it."

There was a slight change in the note of the engine and the floor of the helicopter tilted. Rogo caught the look on the warrant officer's face and said, "Don't try it, bud. Bigger guys than you have been on the end of this."

Rogo chanced a quick glimpse out of the window. The helicopter, he saw, was making a hundred-and-eighty-degree turn. They were doing as he had instructed. With his free arm he wiped the sweat from off his brow.

He motioned his victim to sit down. He backed onto the edge of his own seat, the gun never wavering. The machine had been clattering along for some ten minutes in an oppressive silence when the face of one of the pilots appeared again. *"Ça va?"* he inquired.

Rogo said, "Everything's fine down here. Get me back there and it'll stay that way."

He vanished. The warrant officer eyed Rogo warily and said, "You have made your point with the gun, lieutenant. Do you have to point it at me like that?"

"You'll get an apology from the Police Commissioner about this. I'll see to that. But right now I have no choice. Right?"

Silence again. Then Manny Rosen, who had watched it all with bewilderment, spoke, and Rogo did not try to interrupt him. "Mr. Rogo, I don't understand. You lost your wife, I lost my wife. I know how you feel. I should be back there too. But do you have to threaten people with . . . that thing?"

Rogo looked quickly at the old man and said, "Mrs. Rosen was worth any two of us, Manny. My Linda, goddamn it, you know I'd do anything to get her back. But that's not why I'm going down again. This is no sentimental journey."

There was some sudden chatter in French from the two pilots and immediately Rogo jumped to his feet and put the gun to the officer's head. "What gives?" he growled.

The officer said, "The *Poseidon* is in sight." The helicopter dipped slightly and they could see the ship below. They could also see the small coaster getting closer, the cream yacht appeared to be anchored a mile or so away, and what had been a smudge of smoke on the horizon was now, about five miles distant, a sturdy vessel sprouting whole bouquets of cranes fore and aft.

Steadying himself on the back of the seat, Rogo said, "Tell them to set down nice and soft as near as they can to that hole we came out of. No tricks."

The instructions were relayed in French.

Manny and Martin listened to the exchanges in silence, each confused by swirling eddies of mixed emotions. The fight for survival and the sweet relief of salvation had given way to more complex feelings, and the policeman's superficially crazy wish to return pulled each man's hazy thoughts into sharp focus.

Looking down on the lifeless hulk below, Manny was consumed entirely by what seemed his own betrayal. He had left Belle. No matter that she was dead and this had been his one chance of escape: he had left her. She was down there, marooned among the hideous carnage of the wreck, while he was enjoying the warm security of the helicopter, and the return to normality. It was, quite plainly, an act of betrayal. A lifetime together could not be ended like that. It was too inconclusive. No mourning, no flowers, no elaborate ceremony to signal the passing of a life: no neat severing of the ties of all those shared years. He should have brought her body out with him to give her the dignity of a funeral. His silent sobbing earlier had not been the sign of grief that it appeared. He had been crying for shame, for the wounds of his loss were stinging with the salt of self-disgust.

With Rogo's determination to return, the realization slowly dawned upon Manny that this was his chance to salvage his own sense of honor. He too would return, and bring his beloved Belle out of that hellish wreck.

The little haberdasher also noted with some surprise his own unpredicted reactions. His excited jabbering to the French officer had subsided into a glum silence. It was all over. For a few hours on board the *Poseidon*, James Martin had been a man. A lifetime of being derided, teased, patronized, pitied, and ignored had been suspended for that time. He had faced up to the dangers alongside the more obvious leaders like Scott and Rogo. Despite Rogo's sneering, he had acquitted himself as well as any of them. The many slights that marked his life had been erased. They ran through his mind again now. When the other boys were out in their gangs fishing and climbing trees, James had to stay home and play with the girls. So it had always been for the near invisible man behind a counter in Anaheim: Yes ma'am, and thank you sir, and gee, we're right out of winter scarves. They heard his words and handed him the money, but barely saw the pink-faced salesman. Now the struggles of the past hours had shown him that he had every man's desire to face danger and succeed.

Rogo was going back, Martin did not understand why. But if the adventure was not over, then Martin felt he must play his part in it, as he had done before. For the first time in his life, the man from Anaheim was one of the gang. If Rogo returned, he would too. He rocked forward on his seat and gazed down on the ship. He felt the quickening inside himself. He was excited. The girls and the little boy were sleeping soundly at the back of the helicopter, and he made himself one promise: this time they were not going to leave him with the girls.

Rogo glowered at the three ships within sight of the *Poseidon*, as though he could torpedo them with a look. Still, he thought, they were only like the passersby who tried to muscle in on police action in the streets. He'd move them on when he got down there, and anyway the American authorities were sure to send him help soon.

The warrant officer interrupted his thoughts. "What is it you want us to do exactly?"

"I already told you," Rogo answered steadily. "Land near the hole. I'll jump off. Then get outta here as fast as you can and take these people to safety."

He paused and then added: "Hey, look, I know you guys think I'm crazy but would you do me a favor? Have our embassy guys pass the word back to New York what's happening here? They know what it's all about. Tell them to get the navy here, and fast. Okay?"

The Frenchman saw the open concern on Rogo's face. He gave a curt nod. "They will know soon enough, you may rest assured."

Minutes later, the big machine settled with only the slightest of jerks on the keel. Rogo opened the door and swung out. As his feet touched the wreck, Manny Rosen stood up and said, "I'm going too."

He was out of the door before the astonished policeman could speak.

Rogo grabbed him by the shoulder. He tried one-handed to push Manny back up into the helicopter, but Manny half-wrestled with him and sobbed, "No, Mr. Rogo, please no. My Belle. I can't leave her there. I didn't even say a kaddish."

It was impossible. Rogo could not force him back without hurting him, and he could not bring himself to hit the old man. His face was red with frustration and fury. He let go of him suddenly and scrambled down into the hole in the propeller shaft. As he vanished he shouted to the French crew, "Do what the hell you want with him. He ain't with me."

Manny, puffed from the exertion, looked up in time to see Martin, eyes shining, leap through the door and land beside him. "Hold on, fellas," he cried. "I'm coming too."

The warrant officer looked out on the ludicrous scene. It was beyond all rational explanation. Three rescued men were returning to their highly probable deaths. He tried addressing them calmly. "Listen to me, please, gentlemen. I have not the slightest idea why you are doing this madness. I will help you in any way I can. But if you refuse to come back there is nothing I can do. I am not prepared to be shot trying to save you. I beg you to come now, or we must leave without you. There are the other passengers to consider."

Rogo's face appeared at the hole. It was a gargoyle of rage. "You stupid little jerk! Beat it or I'll put your ass in a sling. You too, Manny. Get out. This has nothing to do with you two!"

Manny did not seem to hear. Martin looked pleadingly at Rogo. "Don't be that way, Mr. Rogo. We were together before. You might need me now."

The crew were talking quickly in French. The warrant officer called for the last time, "We are taking off. Are you coming? Very well." He shook his head, and the door closed. The pilot threw his big blades into gear and the machine lifted and curved off into the distance.

Manny and Martin stood like two schoolboys up before their headmaster. Rogo ran through every obscenity in his considerable vocabulary until at last even his flaming anger burned down. They were here. There was nothing else to be done.

"Okay," he said, stuffing the gun in his pocket and beckoning them on. "You gotta be outta your minds, the two of you, but if that's the way you want, okay. Let's go."

He dropped down again inside the hold, and the others hastened after him.

Other times, other customs. Crime has to be the most modern of industries, and there is no one who takes quicker advantage of the progress of technology than the criminal. So the highwayman has given way to the man with a hand grenade in an airplane, the bank robber has pocketed his gun for the most sophisticated of cutting equipment, and the once furtive cat burglar can now walk in through the front door with his own cut keys.

So the pirate vessel which lay a mile off the wreck of the *Poseidon* that bright morning flew no skull and crossbones, and its crew were far more likely to celebrate a triumph with dry martinis than with rum. The *Naiad*, based at Port Gallice between Cannes and Antibes, was one of the most magnificent private yachts on the Mediterranean. She flew the French flag at her taffrail. She was the property of a handsome playboy by the name of Roland Pascal, in the sense that she was certainly registered in his name. But he, like each of the five young men now so earnestly preparing their scuba-diving equipment on the deck, was helplessly under the sweetly sexual thrall of one silver-haired girl. Heloise, or Hely, as they knew her, was in every sense the captain of that vessel.

Whether a court would have judged them pirates, it would have been hard to know. They harmed no living thing. But in those waters, where fire, explosion, or a mistral was not uncommon, they had no need to trouble the living. They were simply grave robbers, despoilers of the dead. With depth-sounding equipment, underwater metal detectors, the finest diving gear, a decompression chamber, and the most advanced radio equipment, they could follow up any Mayday call or news of disaster at sea.

If this troubled some of the young men, it never worried Hely. Morals, ethics, and scruples did not touch her. They were principles she had jettisoned early in life. Indeed, if she had been born in a state of innocence, it was a condition she had shed almost before leaving the cradle. The smile with which she illuminated some of the smartest parties on the Riviera was the one she had assiduously practiced as a child begging on the streets of Paris, and it earned her an audience now as surely as it had won tourists' pennies twenty years before. The air of innocence had been acquired early too, only now it concealed a past that would make a sailor shudder. As a child she had swiftly digested the cruel lesson that only she could lift herself from the slums to the broad sweet avenues, and that blue eyes and blond hair, properly employed, were potent weapons in that war. By the time she was fifteen she had the skills of the paramour, to which she added the simple but vital insight that has lifted many women to power, that the prince is as easily deceived as his chauffeur, and that all men are equal before a beautiful woman. Via more bedrooms than she could count, Hely had graduated to a luxury yacht on the warm, soft waters of the Mediterranean, and it was here that she held her crew of tough young men so inescapably under her spell that she hardly bothered to conceal the contempt with which she viewed them or, for that matter, any man she had ever met. Hely had come a long way, but she still had a long way to go.

"I wish you wouldn't wear that, Hely." Roland's hesitant request had the faint whine that she had heard so often; sprawled face down on the deck, she did not trouble to turn her head to reply. Instead, she continued to admire the ring on her finger with the diamond the size of an almond. She splayed her fingers and bent her wrist so that the sun caught each shining facet in turn.

"And where do you suggest I should wear it, my love? Outside the headquarters of the Sûreté perhaps? In Cartier's? This is the only place I can wear it."

Roland dropped to his haunches beside her. It was his yacht, she was his girl, but still he could not strike the pleading tone from his voice. "I can still see them, those poor people in that boat." He shuddered. "Doesn't it bother you at all, the thought of that foolish-looking woman floating in front of her dressing-table mirror and the husband still at the wheel?"

Hely lowered her sparkling hand and looked at him. "Was it my fault they were dead? The yacht was listed as missing. We were just lucky to run across it, that's all."

Roland went on, "Her other jewels, the ones we sent to Marseilles, could have finished us. That inquiry came much too close."

Hely ignored him. "I love it!" she cried, raising the diamond to her lips. "I love it, I love it!" A smile sliced across her fine-boned face. "But my poor little Roland? Is he frightened of being a naughty boy then? Is he frightened of being caught playing with the big girls?"

She ceased the mocking irony of the nursery. "Or perhaps it's simply that you no longer find me exciting. Tell me, my lord and master, is that it?" She stirred gently, like a waking cat, and her half-amused eyes saw Roland watching. He would see the ash-blond drape of her hair across the deck, the clean planes of her face, the easy curve of her coppered limbs, and he would crawl. They always did.

"Well, is that it, Roland? Have you found some-one else, someone who doesn't make you be a naughty boy?"

No more than two yards away, the five young men busily sorting out scuba equipment had followed every word, and they mutely acknowledged the nuances of the conversation with winks and grimaces. Roland, acutely aware of their chiding presence, looked anx-ious as he tried to whisper his reply, "You know better than that, Hely. But please listen to me this time. This one is too dangerous. Half the world will be watching soon. We can sail now, and I'll buy you the finest dinner in Athens."

Hely jackknifed to her feet. "There was a time when a good meal could have bought me, but that was long before you, my love. The price is higher now. Today, that's it over there."

She pointed to the dark, lifeless shape of the *Poseidon* clearly defined against the sunlight about a mile distant. Businesslike, she brushed past Roland and addressed herself to the young men scattered around the deck. Each one was in some stage of heaving on diving gear.

"Ready, boys?"

Johnny, the most experienced diver, said, "Yep," cheerfully accepting her authority. He was, he reckoned, running Roland close second in Hely's estimation. She was getting sick of Roland. Soon he would go, and Johnny was all too ready to move in. If that cost him his job, there were plenty more seas for a good scuba man. He shot her his winner's grin.

"Ready for anything with you, Hely." He was gratified to see that his impudent ambiguity was recognized with a slight smile. Any day now, Johnny, he told himself. His confidence and Roland's unease registered with each of the men, and to each it carried the same message: everyone is in with a chance. For Hely, it was a game she had played many times, encouraging, discouraging, a pat here, a slap down there.

She thought, *God, but aren't they like little puppies, each one pushing to the front to be the favorite.*

She addressed them again. "Okay, check your equipment." Two other men, Pierre Duval, the archaeologist, and the captain, Yves, came up from the cabin to watch the final preparations, and Hely gave them their instructions. "Pierre, we won't be needing you. There'll be no pretty statues this time. This one will be for jewelry, and on that wreck there should be enough to . . ."

Johnny picked up her unfinished sentence. "To sink a ship."

Hely's clear, clean laugh would have charmed a country club. "That's right, Johnny, that's right. This is the big one. What extraordinary luck. Think of it. A few minutes after midnight on New Year's Eve. They would all be together in the main dining room, wearing their silly hats, rattling noisemakers, and throwing streamers and confetti at each other, joining arms and singing 'Auld Lang Syne.' " Her voice drifted off and arms again wandered to the distant hulk. "Gala night. Black ties, long dresses. And fat old bags wearing their once-a-year finest, rings, necklaces, bracelets, all the prizes their dull little husbands paid for in ulcers. All we have to do is go and collect."

Roland's protesting hand fell feebly from her arm as she took three quick steps towards the neatly stacked wet suits and equipment. She flipped off her bikini top and, palms on thighs, slid her shorts to the deck as though she were the only person on the entire ocean. Every man there watched in silence, and noticed the slim scarf of untanned white between the oak-brown back and legs. If she sensed the silence, she gave no indication of it, and continued her briefing.

"We will approach the ship from the opposite side of that freighter and descend to the level of the dining room. Inside, we must all work quickly."

One of the divers asked, "Will we need spear guns?"

Hely curtly replied, "No. And don't waste time on junk. You all know decent pieces when you see them. Necklaces first, then brooches, bracelets, and rings." She stooped to pick up her wet suit.

The excitement she had engendered amongst the divers was almost an audible hum. A boy of eighteen who only six months earlier had been expelled from his English public school exchanged winks with a young Frenchman, who then mimed a silent whistle. Johnny, arrested in some discomfort with his arms halfway through the straps of his oxygen kit, contemplated a delightful future. The already discomfited Roland had been rendered speechless by her display of nonchalant sexuality, and it was only the whispered reactions of the men beside him that jolted him, so that he interrupted her with hissing urgency, "For God's sake, Hely, can't you change in the cabin?"

He regretted it the moment she turned her head and he saw the coolly amused eyes through the thistledown hair. "Roland thinks I'm upsetting you boys. Are there any complaints?" For Roland's benefit, she indicated their whooped denials and half cheers with a tilt of her head, and stepped into her wet suit. She rolled it up without hurry and was zipping up the front when she faced Roland and resumed. "Roland, darling, I'm worried. I'm beginning to think there's just the faintest aroma of chicken about you, *mon amour*. And now you seem ashamed to let people see me."

Roland tried for a cheery grin that emerged more as a wince. Johnny thought, *He's cracking.*

Roland said, "Hasn't it occurred to you that you are corrupting these more or less decent young men?"

Hely picked up her oxygen cylinders and looped the first strap over her arm. She replied, "Oh yes, I know that, Roland. But isn't it fun? Well, isn't it, boys?"

Johnny led the cheering that greeted her question as Hely went on, "But don't come if you don't want to, Roland. Perhaps little Bobby here will hold my hand if I get nervous."

The young Englishman started at the sound of his name. He promised, "There and back, Hely," and Hely noted with satisfaction the brief scowl that touched Johnny's lips at the encouragement of another contender.

Hely resumed her instructions. "Oh, and another thing. Those bodies have been in there eight hours or so and their fingers might be swollen. Don't waste time wrestling." She slipped her diver's knife from the sheath she was strapping to her leg and made a small dropping motion with the blade that required no explanation. Grins gone, the diving crew agreed with somber nods.

"I'll come." Roland's statement was flat and his face pale and grim, but Hely rewarded him with a birthday smile that seemed to belie all her earlier goading. "I didn't like this from the start, when we heard the Mayday call. But I'll come."

It's so easy, she thought. The lessons of the slums operated with the same efficacy here or anywhere. She had administered the scare that Roland needed. She had teasingly half-promised Johnny, and then, when he became a little too confident, pushed him down a couple of rungs and warmed up the English boy. If they all died tomorrow, she thought, she would not waste a second's grief on them. They were men, just men, easily found, easily fooled, easily dropped, and there was a whole world full of them. Then the old thought, the one that sometimes troubled her, swam into her mind. Was there one man in the whole world who was worthy of her respect? Even more, was there one man who could inspire in her the pathetic combination of adoration and lust which she saw in the faces around her? She provided herself with the answer, as she always did. No. Never. Even if there was, Hely's ascent from the gutter to the stars could not be slowed for so intangible and profitless a business as love. It was an emotion that was best left to shopgirls in their blind dash to the miseries of motherhood that always ended in ugly, corseted middle age and anxiety over paying the rent. For Hely, the supreme emotion was power.

She twisted the heavy ring off her finger and handed it to Yves. "Look after this for me, will you, Yves? Pierre will stay with you. We have an hour and a half of air. I don't expect any complications. We will return before the time is up. If we do not, we have encountered something unexpected. Give us an extra ten minutes, and after that you are under orders to up anchor and get out." She looked at Roland sweetly and added, "Where do you suggest, darling? Morocco? Tunis? Algeria? I should think they wouldn't ask too many questions in Algeria."

Gratefully Roland grabbed the chance to exert at least half his authority, and agreed, "Algeria, I would think. Sell the yacht and split what you can get."

Hely's beam of warm approbation swept the semi-circle of men as they rose to their feet, oxygen cylinders in place, flippers on feet. "Good. *Allons!* Hely's Heroes swim at five meters below the surface."

It was Hely who was the first to drop her face mask and slip over the side, and as the six other divers in their impersonal black uniforms followed, their thoughts shared a highly personal but also uniform vision. Glittering jewels dancing in the light, and a silky ribbon wrapped round a brown body.

Klaas himself took the wheel to bring the *Magt* up under the lee of the wreck. It was eight-thirty in the morning. Then he handed it over to Piet, and climbed down to join Jason and Coby on the deck.

"Did you send the wire?" Jason asked.

Klaas nodded. He produced the sheet of paper from his pocket and read out loud: "Today, January first at eight twenty-seven, I, Captain Klaas van Zeevogel, master of the fifteen-hundred-ton freighter *Magt van Leiden* registered in Amsterdam, have made fast a line to the wreck of the *Poseidon*. I hereby claim rights of prime salvor."

"Great," Jason grinned. "That's a smart move, Klaas. If you can't help anyone here, you might as well have the benefit of salvage rights."

"Possibly." Klaas was not too enthusiastic. "It is a precaution, I suppose. But what really concerns me, Jason, is why that helicopter returned and those men got out. I think there were three."

A frown also crossed Jason's face, "I made it three too. I don't get it. What makes survivors come back to a sinking ship? And one of them, that guy in the undershirt, looked like a cop to me."

"You can tell a cop at that distance in the middle of the ocean?" Klaas looked even more worried.

"I could recognize a cop on a dark night in China," Jason said. He saw the older man's concern and clapped him on the shoulder. "Don't worry, Klaas. If he is a cop he'll keep an eye on me for you."

The Dutchman looked up at the tall young man. "Frankly, Jason, I am not happy about the whole thing. I think it is about time you told us of your business on board this vessel too."

The American's face tightened as Coby echoed her father's request. "Please tell us," she said.

Jason moved to the deck rail, weighing in his hand a grappling iron on a length of nylon line. With a steady overarm swing he sent the iron lobbing through the air and over the hoisting bracket above the propeller.

"First time!" he called over his shoulder. He tugged the rope sharply, several times. It was secure.

Then he faced them again and said, "I told you. I have business on the *Poseidon*. One small part of that cargo belongs to me, and I'm going to have it. That may be enough for you, it may not, but it's all I can tell you. Beyond that you've got to trust me."

Almost too quickly, Coby came back, "We do, don't we, papa?"

After a lifetime at sea, Klaas was not a man who made decisions based on flimsy facts. He liked the man. He liked the look of him, the set of him, and the way he handled himself around a boat. But he was still only a stranger they had plucked off the sea's surface. He pushed back the cap on his graying, springy hair and the bewilderment was there, plainly registered on his face.

"I shall wait and see, Captain Jason. I hope I shall not be disappointed."

Jason was leaning back on the line, testing its hold by bracing one leg against the side of the *Poseidon*. "It's a fairly straight walk up to the top where those other guys got in. Let's go see what gives in there."

The Dutchman moved across and touched his sleeve. Klaas said, "Well? Will I be disappointed?"

With no more effort than he would make to walk across the deck, Jason moved quickly up the line, legs stiff against the hull, hands working alternately. He was near the top when his answer carried down, "It's a disappointing world, Captain Klaas."

Klaas shrugged his shoulders at Coby. What was he to think? He had asked the man for some sort of promise, and been repaid with cynical flippancy. There was too much mystery here. He did not like mysteries. The whispering men in waterfront bars who wanted undisclosed consignments dropped off near the coast at night. Nameless passengers who wished to travel without the formalities of customs and passports. Klaas had turned his back on them all. His workworn freighter with its limping engine provided him with an honest, uncomplicated trade that matched his nature. Jason and his mysteries could only mean trouble.

"Please, papa." Coby had followed his tumbling doubts. "He is a good man, I know it. Please?"

Klaas struggled with three emotions, his life-long instinct to avoid trouble, his love for his daughter, and a curious but irritating doubt that he might have misjudged the American. They looked up and saw Jason astride the propeller-shaft housing. "Hey, there. Come on up here, and bring the rope ladder and the lanterns with you. Or do you need a bosun's chair?"

Klaas stuffed his pipe into his pocket, and tucked the ready-rolled rope ladder under his arm. "Who does he think I am—Rip Van Winkle?" Coby's relieved laughter followed him up the rope. The possibility that there might still be people to be saved on board had tilted the balance in his mind. But, with every heave of his hands, he thought, *Klaas van Zeevogel, you are becoming careless and stupid in your old age.*

Coby had no such doubts. She loved her days on the *Magt*, she loved the sea, and she loved her father. But the excitement that boiled inside her came from the man with one name who had just sailed into her life. She felt the clean, unquestioning confidence in this shining new emotion that dies at the first lie, the first deceit, the first mistake. She knew, and that was more than enough. She wriggled up after them, and when Jason's arm around her shoulder steadied her for a second all her shapeless fantasies merged into one face.

Klaas began to lower himself into the opening in the propeller-shaft housing. He said, "Now we shall see what hidden treasure lures survivors back to a sinking ship."

Jason grunted agreement, but his eyes were on the *Komarevo*'s industrious approach in the distance. He was more concerned to know what hidden treasure there was aboard the *Poseidon* that would interest Captain Ilich Bela, and how many bodies he was prepared to step over this time to get to it.

MINDING THE STORE

4

The fear which had spurred them in their climb up the tangled mountain of wreckage when they were fleeing the ship had gone; now the three survivors struggled laboriously down to the ceiling which had become the floor of the inverted engine room. Without the adrenaline fired by that terror, they saw all too clearly the drop beneath them to the saw-edged wreckage of the gigantic machinery. Turbines, dynamos, reduction gearing, everything of any size and weight, torn away from its bolts, now lay in tangled turmoil below, and Martin whistled his shocked surprise when he realized what they had achieved. Manny saw nothing but the shadowed corner by the pool where he had left his wife's body.

Rogo refused to look down to the silent pool where Linda and Scott had both died. He was the cop again, back on the job. "C'mon you guys, move it." It was the first lesson learned in a street accident: keep 'em moving. Driven by his words, they edged out into the crazily distorted web of metal which had been their final ascent to salvation. The lighter metalwork of the room, the platforms and handrails and catwalks and steps, remained, but they had been smashed into an erratic lacework pattern that stretched from the curved, studded interior of the hull to the jungle of shattered machinery and weird pools that was now the floor. First James Martin, then Manny Rosen, and finally Rogo moved step by cautious step across and down the mutilated scaffolding. Manny, his eyes still searching for his wife's body, lost his footing on a catwalk greased with the oil that coated almost every surface. For a moment he teetered on one leg, hands frantically scrambling in the air for a hold; the rock-solid arm of Rogo caught him.

Rogo thought, *Cripples! A deal like this and what am I stuck with? A couple of goddamn cripples!*

He repeated it to himself when a handrail which Martin was testing broke the half-shorn bolt that held it, and went spinning into the abyss. The sharp clang of its landing echoed through the cathedral-like vault.

It was only when they reached the bottom that Rogo took in the scene to which duty had recalled him. Belle Rosen's body was slumped, lifelessly draped without dignity among the girders, at the spot where she had sacrificed her life to save theirs. Beside her was the small pool which filled the stairway leading to the rest of the ship. Beyond it lay the larger pool which had swallowed the Reverend Scott and Linda Rogo.

Rogo's breath rasped from the climb down. The only other sound was the drip of oil and water, and the occasional creak of the deformed metalworks. It was a fearful sight, made more so by the similarity in space and sound to a church. Each drip chimed like a bell around the huge hollow of the boat's stern. The smaller pool gave off a haunted glow from what little light penetrated the waters from the corridors beyond. The bigger pool, which led through a huge curved cylinder to the funnel, was still, and black, and evil smelling.

The air was not the wholesome chill of the sea, but a foul stench that came from the hideous mélange created by the capsize. Rogo knew those ingredients only too well. Oil and water, food and drink, every substance from the captain's unfinished martini to the contents of the washrooms had gone into that vile broth, together with the bodies of sixteen hundred people. They were standing in a waterlogged coffin, and the stench of death was everywhere. He understood how Manny felt. Rogo's firsthand experience of death as a policeman had long since swept away any sentimentality he might have felt, but he could still comprehend Manny's determination to rescue his wife's body. It was Belle's supreme act of courage that had enabled them to escape. Throughout their long climb up through the bowels of the wrecked ship she had been apologizing for her weight, her lack of agility, and the way she had slowed them down. She had even offered to stay behind. But then had come her moment. When Scott was trapped in the underwater dive that would lead them into the engine room, Belle Rosen, former swimming champion, had dived in to rescue him. It had been too much for her heart. They had been saved, and they had left her there. Even to Rogo that seemed unjust.

Rogo shook himself. He'd a job to do, and Mike Rogo didn't leave business unfinished. Even so, his single-mindedness wavered when he looked at his two companions. Christ! A storekeeper who behaves like he's at summer camp and a heartbroken old Jew. Rogo's team! The New York Mets it ain't, Rogo thought. Two guys in tuxedos and evening dress pants, caked in filth and oil and half-beat with exhaustion, looking as though they're going to break into a dance and sing "We're a Couple of Swells," and himself in an undershirt and pants like an engineer's rag. They wouldn't serve them a beer in a trucker's bar.

He stood on the surer ground of the girders and wide steel plates that surrounded the small pool and spread his arms out. "Welcome home, fellas!" he roared.

Manny was kneeling beside his dead wife. He had hurried to her as soon as they had completed the climb down. Tears painted white paths on his oil-dark face, and sobs came unhindered from his lips.

"Mamma, oh Mamma, oh Mamma." Over and over again, he repeated it. "I came back for you, didn't I? You knew I would. You knew your Manny wouldn't leave you. When did I ever leave you, huh? That time you had the operation, who was it stayed with you and fixed the food and everything? So don't worry, Mamma, everything's going to be fine."

He dropped his face into his hands and whimpered like a child. Then he fell silent, and lowered his hands and looked at her again. Their lives had been inextricably interwoven almost every minute for forty years. In the hardware shop they had served at the counter side by side. "Pass me those mops, will you, Belle?" "Hey, Manny, would you get me the knife-sharpeners down, the doctor says I mustn't reach too high?" In the evenings they would sit together, or visit relatives together, or maybe go to a movie together. But always together. She called herself "a real home person" and was a little proud that, unlike some wives, she didn't race around the coffee morning circuit or to card evenings. Manny had never been a man to go out for a beer with the boys, or even a walk around the block alone. That sort of mutual dependence never ends, not even with death.

Manny Rosen had known his wife was dead, but the irreversible finality of it had not reached him until now. She *was* dead. What he saw here was only a corpse and his beloved Mamma existed only in his memory. His hand went to the medallion she had won for swimming as Belle Zimmerman. She had asked him to deliver it to their little grandson in Israel. That was what he must do.

But first he must take Belle from this evil place and see her buried with honor and dignity. He rose slowly from his knees, for the first time conscious of his new role: widower.

"Mr. Rogo," he said. The sobbing had left his voice now. "Mr. Rogo, I think I'd like to take Belle away from here now, if that's okay with you."

Rogo looked at the shambling figure, and it was only the clear sincerity in the bereaved man's voice that checked his hair-trigger temper. Manny plainly knew what he must do, but in his confusion and distress he had not for a second begun to consider how it could be done.

"Yeah, just like that." Rogo immediately regretted the hurtful irony in his tone. "Look, Manny," he began to explain, "this ain't New York. You can't just whistle a goddamn cab or hop a subway. If we get a chance to get Belle outta here, then great."

He became more serious, and threw a finger like a truncheon first at Manny, then at Martin. "But get this straight. You two guys jumped in on my deal. Nobody asked you along, right? You gotta stay to the end, and that's when I say."

Manny's eyes had dropped. "I'm sorry, Mr. Rogo. I guess I'm not thinking straight. I'll go along with what you say." He looked around helplessly as he realized for the first time the illogicality of Rogo's return. "But why did you come back? I don't understand it."

Martin cut in, "That's right. If we're going to help you, and we are a kind of a team by now, you've got to tell us what ball game we're in."

Rogo felt a leaden weariness in his limbs, and sat down slowly on one of the girders.

He said, "Okay fellas, okay."

Rogo was not a man who was often assailed by doubts. He liked the old familiar problems, where his rudimentary sense of justice and bulldozing tactics were ideal. "I get a call to a bar mebbe. I go in. There's a guy pulled a knife. I hit him with a chair and kick him in the nuts. That's my job." That was what he said when people asked him what he did. It was simple, it was effective, and in his eyes it seemed more or less fair. Here, it seemed, his whole world had been turned upside down with the ship.

There was no identifiable enemy. There was no one to hit.

It had been his reward. "Straightforward security job," they had told him. "One dollar, one hundred dollars, it's the same. Sit on your ass and enjoy the sun, Mike." That's what they said. He should have stuck to barroom brawls.

He nodded his head across the dark vault of the room. Beyond the small pool, the pale light that crept through their escape opening was augmented by the two lanterns they had carried down, and it turned the snarled rails and pipes of the terrible debris into a delicate silver filigree through which they could see a high steel bulkhead.

He spoke in a passionless, flat voice. "There's a special hold over there, like a goddamn big wall safe. Inside there's half a billion dollars in gold bars. I'm here to keep the mice away."

For a whole minute the only sound was the steady, distant dripping.

Then Martin's excitement bubbled over into words, "That's a lot of dough!"

Rogo's face lifted. He replied, "You'd have to sell a helluva lot of socks in Anaheim for that."

Manny asked quietly, "How'd it come about, one cop in charge of all that . . . gold?"

Rogo ran through it virtually verbatim from the endless briefings he had before the cruise. "Our honeymoon was a cover for the five of us. Moscowitz was a steward, Riley in the pantry, Ruffallo in the boiler room, Petersen played deckhand. I was the guy in the monkey suit amongst the passengers."

He scraped up a morsel of hostility. "On account of my exquisite table manners." He smiled at his own joke, then continued. "They're all dead. That leaves me, and that's why I couldn't quit."

Martin asked, "I don't mean to sound rude, Mr. Rogo, but why would they have, well, y'know, ordinary cops on a job like this?"

"I guess I've been long enough on Broadway to smell a bribe. This stuff is packed in cases marked Toledo Wire and Bolt Company of which there ain't none. Hush money, payoff money, setup money, it's all the same. Nowadays you can square anybody with money and that goes for governments and big business too. All I know is someone in Athens was going to make the pickup and no announcements in the newspapers. So they asked a bunch of lame-brain cops. Ain't you read the papers lately? The CIA is down the can, the FBI is busted up. They don't trust the Treasury spooks no more. They reckoned they could find five honest cops on the New York force. If they'd wanted six they might've been in trouble."

The sheer scale of the problem threw a depressed silence over the three men. Even so, Martin tried to spring back. "Well," he said, "I guess we've got to sit it out."

It was vague, but at least it was hopeful, and Rogo recovered a little of his spirit. "Yeah," he agreed. "They gotta send someone soon. If this old scow can stay afloat a few hours longer, there'll be a couple of destroyers alongside, and when they come they'll find Rogo minding the store."

The three were scrambling over the debris towards the hold when a lancing beam froze them like scarecrows in its piercing light. From the blackness behind it, high in the roof, a voice called down, "Get the coffee out, boys, you got company." It was an American voice.

"What did I tell you?" Rogo whooped. "They're here!"

Life rarely disturbed the composure of the elegant captain of the salvage vessel *Komarevo*, and when his first mate excitedly pointed out the activity around the upturned shell of the *Poseidon*, Captain Bela adjusted the cigar between teeth that would have done credit to a Hollywood dentist, and corrected the exposure of his cuffs. It was, by his standards, a display of considerable emotion. Indeed, those who had known Captain Bela for many years were hard pressed to recall anything that had ever shaken the equanimity of a man who had no difficulty in reconciling the most optimistic side of Marxism with the opportunism of Al Capone. Captain Bela delighted in his own contradictions. He was a Bulgarian, but the flag over the stern of his twenty-five-hundred-ton salvage vessel bore the convenient emblems of Panama. He was a committed Communist, but his six-figure savings were in a numbered account with a Swiss bank. He could talk of the triumph of the proletariat while complaining of any caviar other than beluga, and the shirts he ordered by the half-dozen from Paris were, he assured his more Party-conscious friends, merely sentimental souvenirs of the last days of capitalism. He had the manners of a duke, played a fine hand of bridge, and his skills equaled his very considerable charm. He was a bachelor, but Captain Ilich Bela spent few solitary nights.

He was also as deadly as a cobra.

Self-assurance shone from his lean, handsome features as he surveyed the scene from the bridge of the *Komarevo*. His cap, with its gold badge insignia, was set at a formally horizontal angle, and the four stripes on his sleeve confirmed an authority reflected in his every action.

The *Komarevo* plowed through still seas at a businesslike twelve knots towards the *Poseidon*, now a swiftly diminishing two miles distant. Through Zeiss binoculars that had once decorated the chest of a German U-boat commander, Captain Bela examined the inverted hull carefully, and then swung the glasses to look again at the *Naiad*, a little over a mile away, completing a rough triangle on the mirror surface of the sea. He hummed a note of mild interest as he watched the minuscule black figures swarm over the side.

Beside him the first mate wrinkled his gorilla features in incomprehension at the contented smile on his captain's face.

"See, captain!" he cried. His arm, as thick as a tree, swept to include the freighter on the starboard side of the *Poseidon* and the yacht lazing in the sun. "People here before us. Not good, eh?"

Captain Bela's look of gratified tranquility did not diminish. He moved to the wing of the bridge and examined the scene and, again touching one cuff, replied to his waiting lieutenant. "Not good, you think, Anton. No, not good. Excellent! One might almost say perfect."

He stepped through the door from the bridge into the cabin, and picking up a magnifying glass confirmed their respective positions on the chart on the table. Anton's bulk filled the doorway and threw a large shadow across the chart. His over two hundred pounds of muscle had many applications in his captain's interest, but planning strategy was not amongst them. His small, ratlike eyes watched patiently from the fleshy face, and his thickly padded fingers drummed heavily on the door frame as he waited for the explanation.

Captain Bela put down the magnifying glass. "Ah, Anton, my dear fellow, I hardly know where I would be without you. But I have warned you before about the dangers of thinking too much.

"You are worried about what we have seen, right? Three men, we must assume survivors, have returned from the helicopter to the ship for God knows what reason. A broken-down coaster has put a line aboard her, presumably hoping to claim salvage rights. And a pleasure yacht crewed by amateur thieves has come to take a look. Oh yes, I know the *Naiad* all right. They are the pickpockets of the ocean. It is my business to know about such people."

Anton thrust a thick finger into his ear, pulled it out, and reviewed the result with some pleasure. "But they're all here before us," he repeated.

There was a discernible sigh in the captain's voice as he resumed, "Quite so, Anton, they are here before us. Let them be first. Let them go about their business. Then we shall move in, which is a great deal better than having them interrupt us at our business. Since the freighter is apparently an honest ship, we must point out that we are much better equipped for such a task, that authority is vested in us from Athens, and that life might become difficult for them if they were to get in our way. The three men must leave on the freighter since they cannot have any conceivable right to be on board. And the petty pilferers from the *Naiad*? We should not be doing our duty, Anton, if we did not dispose of them permanently."

Anton's broken teeth emerged in a smile that spread across his flat, battered face. Disposal was his territory. "Kill them, captain?"

"Certainly, Anton. We owe it to the world. And the world will thank us for making the seas safe for honest sailors."

His voice took on a more purposeful tone. "Take these instructions. There is a diving job to be done. The *Naiad* has six or seven scuba divers down and they will almost certainly be heading for the main dining room to rob the dead. Tell Hugo to take nine divers, with spear guns and knives, and lose them. It should not pose any problems. They are children in these matters. I will deal with the freighter and those three men."

Captain Bela hummed a jaunty tune and strolled back onto the bridge as Anton lurched down the companionway to deliver his instructions. Ilich Bela was a happy man. It was a tricky job, but he had the crew and the vessel to accomplish it, and if there was an opportunity to exercise his own ingenuity and capacity for violence, then so much the better. Captain Bela enjoyed a challenge. His crew of Iron Curtain thugs was unquestionably well qualified in all matters of brute force, up to and including murder. His vessel, its decks packed with cranes and hoists and booms, was admirably suited to the work of quickly shifting and carrying unspecified cargo. There were few illegal seafaring missions that the *Komarevo* had not undertaken in the last three years, and Captain Bela had the pleasing thought that those operations had almost been rehearsals for this, the one major strike that would assure his future. He and his boat had delivered guns to people of every political and criminal persuasion. They had transported passengers without passports from one country to another without benefit of immigration authorities. They had recovered sunken ships and lost cargo that were registered with no insurance company. They had staged funerals at sea at night without the ceremony of the last rites. His employers in Athens had told him that the cargo was gold, held in a special hold off the engine room, that it had to be recovered swiftly and silently, and Captain Ilich Bela knew with cold certainty that a very considerable percentage of that gold would stay with the man who recovered it.

He indulged in speculation as he watched the *Komarevo*'s determined bow cut through the water. An apartment in Nice would be convenient. Those French girls: even a good Communist must bow occasionally to human frailties. He would have to keep the Lamborghini there, of course, for it was one of the minor irritations of revolution that even half a century later it had not lost its puritanical zeal. What was it he always said when his Western friends queried his excellent if expensive tastes? "Comrades, I would dearly love to wear a hair shirt, but they are always so dreadfully cut." Bela's slim fingers again checked his cuff, and he was making a mental note to speak to his shirtmaker about sleeve lengths, when the plump young radio operator came puffing up the steps to the bridge.

Bela took the decoded message from his hand and read it with a slight frown. More to himself than to anyone, he said, "Do we know a Detective Lieutenant Michael Rogo? I can't imagine that we do. Whoever he is, our friends in Athens are most concerned that he should not appear on the survivors' list." The world, as far as Captain Bela was concerned, would be none the worse with one less policeman of any nationality.

"And tell Anton," he told the radio operator, "to stand off one hundred meters. We shall board her in the pinnace, and he is to hold that distance until our return."

Captain Bela raised the binoculars once again. No, there was nothing on that half-sunken ruin that the *Komarevo* could not handle, and although the smooth young Bulgarian had many reservations about the Americans as a people they did occasionally find exactly the right phrase for a situation.

"Like shooting fish in a rain barrel," he said aloud, and the *Komarevo*, its engines drumming solidly, a plume of black smoke lying behind in the windless air, headed for the scene.

The tired figures around the table in the Athens office stood to attention when Stasiris came bustling into the room. They had been there over six hours now. Jackets were off, ties undone, and dress shirts were rumpled and stained. Their faces, without exception, were drawn with weariness and distress.

"Gentlemen, we have news." Stasiris wagged a sheaf of wire messages.

"Has it sunk?" The questioner did not attempt to conceal his hope.

"I fear not," Stasiris replied. "The *Poseidon* is still

afloat, down by the bow, keel up, about two-thirds submerged."

The questioner dropped his head into his hands.

"There are other developments." Stasiris continued in his impersonal, businesslike manner. "Three of the survivors have returned to the wreck."

"Returned?" Several voices repeated the same word.

The president looked around the group. "One of them . . ." he consulted a paper, ". . . a detective lieutenant of the New York police named Michael Rogo, and two other men."

The bleary-eyed faces were blank with astonishment. "Why?" one member asked. "Why did they go back?"

Stasiris' upturned palms showed he had no answer. "This confounded detective has complicated everything. Bela will be almost there now and we could have kept the whole operation quiet. I instructed him to salvage the . . . the cargo, if possible, and if not, sink it. Now he has this policeman round his neck, and if this Rogo fellow gets off alive we cannot stop him talking."

He sighed heavily and continued. "Again I have had to act and I seek your approval. I have spoken to New York, and they are, as you can imagine, no happier than we are about this. I suggested, and they agreed, that we give Bela carte blanche. I have therefore already wired him that complete security must be maintained." He looked round the room and added quietly, "At any price."

The man who had been drunk a few hours earlier was sober now. He looked at Stasiris warily. "If you mean what I think you mean . . ."

Pularnos intervened. "I do not think there is any need to spell it out. We are talking about international security now. I must ask you to consider how you would balance the life of a single American policeman against the possibility of war."

A messenger entered the room and padded silently to Stasiris. The president took the slip of paper, put his hand over his eyes, and groaned.

"What is it?" Pularnos asked urgently.

"As if matters were not complicated enough," he replied. "A Dutch freighter got a line on the *Poseidon* first and is claiming salvage rights."

Half rising, Pularnos protested, "We cannot allow that."

"We cannot disallow it," Stasiris snapped, writing his acknowledgment on the bottom of the message. "Without wishing to take you through the mysteries of salvage law, his claim as prime salvor is irrefutable."

He rose. "Now, gentlemen, I suggest we all go and make ourselves look a little more civilized and reassemble here as soon as possible. We can do nothing for the moment."

Their counterparts in New York had just been through an almost identical explanation from Mr. Arthur Haven. He stubbed out a cigar in an overloaded ashtray and added, "Athens has their guy out there, and we can only hope he can do the job."

The Secretary of Defense was looking out of the window over the scattered lights of New York. "That doesn't sound so damned hot to me, Arthur," he said. "A strong-arm collector of Broadway whores and pimps muscling in on this sort of sensitive deal— my God, if he talks the whole thing blows sky high." He turned his back on the New York night and added,

"And who the hell is this character the Greeks are using anyway?"

Haven looked at the papers before him. "Bela," he said. "A Captain Ilich Bela. He is described to me as a man of unbridled violence."

One of the disheveled figures at the table straightened suddenly. "Hey, now look here, Arthur, I'm not going to be party to having a slug put into a New York cop."

Haven's calm exterior exploded. "No one is asking you to be party to anything, you goddamn clown! This Bela is going in there and he's going to fix it so that no one will be any the wiser. Right, Mr. Secretary?"

The politician agreed. "None of us need know what happens aboard that damned ship. All we need concern ourselves with is that the contents are never known. Don't forget, if we can't get this shipment through to the Greek Cypriots, the U.S. government might want to set the whole thing up again. I shall also arrange for one of our security men in Athens to get hold of this bull-headed interfering cop *if* he should return."

The original questioner still looked unconvinced. "Call it any name you like, it's gangsterism," he said.

Haven raised an eyebrow. "The name is politics, Ed. It's one cop, or Greece and Turkey at each other's throats and the NATO alliance in pieces. Think about it. Now let's break it up, boys. I'll have a call put out for you the minute we hear any more."

UNDER THE CHRISTMAS TREE

5

The three survivors had waited for what seemed like divine deliverance as the two lights had rocked down the scaffolding of the pipes towards them. Hope degenerated into uncertainty as they saw only three figures, and finally, for Rogo at least, into blazing disgust as he contemplated his rescuers. A young chick, an old seaman, and what looked to his eyes suspiciously like one of those kooks who waved banners.

He reverted to the police manual. "Detective Lieutenant Rogo, Thirty-eighth Precinct, New York Police Department," he said. "Now just what the hell do you guys think you're doing here?"

The older man stepped forward. "Captain Klaas van Zeevogel, commander of the coaster *Magt van Leiden*. We have a line on board this vessel, which gives us prime salvage rights. Perhaps you could explain what you are doing so far from home, officer."

Rogo replied, "Damn right I will. The three of us survived when this tub turned over. I'm on a security job and I'm sitting watchdog on this cargo. And what I don't want right now is the Swiss Family Robinson walking all over my patch." He flicked a dismissive hand at the unlikely trio.

He spoke to the Dutchman, but his eyes were on the younger man, who had detached himself from the other two, strolled to one side and was now leaning against a steel tank.

"You see my position," Klaas went on. "You are now, in the eyes of the courts, a trespasser, and have no rights on board this vessel at all."

The younger man was brushing his lower lip with his thumbnail with a gesture that stood halfway between boredom and amusement. *He's the one to watch*, thought Rogo. He replied, "You're not the first guy to try to tell me the law, little man."

Klaas looked slightly shocked. "I'm afraid that is the position. Under maritime salvage laws, rights to inspect or remove cargo belong to the first salvor on the scene, and that is myself. The owners of the ship have acknowledged my position."

His nervousness was showing and Rogo decided to bulldoze him. "I don't give a monkey's ass if the Rams' front four acknowledged your position. The only inspecting and removing around here is going to be done by me, and no guy who runs trips around the bay tells me different." He jabbed a finger at Jason. "And who's this you dragged along?"

More uncertain, Klaas said, "He is a yachtsman who capsized west of here. His name is Jason, he has a captain's ticket, and he's going to Athens."

Rogo asked, "Then why doesn't he just keep right on going?"

Klaas wavered, then said, "He claims he has business aboard the *Poseidon*."

"Is that so?" Rogo folded his arms. "What's the business, pal?"

Thumbs hooked in the top of his jeans, Jason grinned, "Private, Batman, private."

Rogo advanced one step towards Jason. "You look like you're on private business. I roll you guys off the park bench every night. The only business you guys know is busting the coin-box on slot machines. I don't like freaks, mister."

The grin flashed back on Jason's face. "Sorry you don't like my appearance, officer. But I sure do admire your disguise."

Everyone looked at Rogo. His dignity had quite suddenly gone. He was a middle-aged, unshaven, overweight man, filthy dirty and wearing only an undershirt and grimy trousers. Klaas saw Rogo's eyes begin to pop, and started, "Gentlemen, I'm sure there's no need . . ." But Rogo's hand came out of his pocket. He was holding his gun and it was pointing at Jason. Rogo was solving it the only way he understood.

"That's enough, funny guy," he bellowed. "You're going to tell me what the hell this business of yours is and then you're going to move your ass offa this boat."

The gun did not appear to register with Jason. He

simply said, "Not a chance, not a chance. Now what do you do? Shoot me or book me?"

As Rogo's frustrated tongue stumbled, Martin decided to help. "You should listen to Mr. Rogo," he told Jason. "He really is an important police officer. It's just that we all got, well, kinda mussed up trying to get out. But he's on a real big-time security job here looking after half a billion dollars in gold."

His keen little face searched around for the reaction to this information. He didn't see Rogo's hand until it grabbed the front of his tattered dress shirt and heaved him up onto his toes.

"Martin, what'd you do with your brains—sell 'em with those goddamn socks?"

Martin's chin strained. Through trapped teeth he mumbled, "Gee, I'm sure sorry, Mr. Rogo. I was only trying to help."

Rogo's fist opened and Martin fell like a sack. Rogo's venom again faded. It was all too much. Take a rest, they had told him. Take Linda along with you. No one will know a thing, and all you have to do is to keep an eye on it. Go and sit in the sun, Rogo, they had said, and try to keep your hands off the belly dancers. Rogo spat into the pool. He said, "For Chrissakes!" but without real enthusiasm.

"Is that true?" Jason's smile had gone.

"Yep." Rogo was, temporarily at least, defused. "It's true, okay. It's in there." He indicated the hold with a weary wave of the gun. All security had gone now.

Jason said, "Okay, then listen to me. We don't have much time. This ship can't stay afloat forever. She's one-third clear of the water, there must still be quite a lot of air trapped down there, but we can't be more than a couple of hours. Captain Klaas here, whether you like it or not, does have full authority to exercise salvage rights on this ship. That needn't concern you. Klaas is a straight man. Look at him, for God's sake. You're supposed to be a cop, you should know an honest face when you see one. He's not interested in trying to get his hands on government money of any kind. Right, Klaas?"

The Dutchman nodded. "I'm sure we can agree that you must continue your security operation, lieutenant. That sort of . . . well, extraordinary consignment is outside my scope, I assure you."

Jason continued, "So you sit on your crock of gold and let Klaas go ahead with normal salvage work."

It sounded reasonable. Rogo weighed it all very carefully. The Dutchman was a captain. Rogo's faith in the integrity of a uniform and peaked cap was considerable. And the freak was at least American.

He spoke to Jason. "What about you? You tell me what your stake is and we got a deal."

They all waited. Klaas juggled with his puzzle: if the man was honest, why wouldn't he explain himself? This stupid argument was wasting time; the ship could go down at any moment, and they must act quickly and leave. Coby prayed that he would say something, anything, so that they would believe in him as she did. Manny wished this difficult man would declare himself so that they could leave this stinking cavern and the cold crumpled body that had been his wife. Martin, who had always believed in the authority of a clean collar and a regular change of underwear, wondered how it could be that such a shabby figure could command their attention and only wished he could do the same.

Rogo had a rough grasp of crowd psychology. He knew how to move them on, how to make the loud-mouths back down. He had disliked this man on sight. His style was too close to that of the longhairs he despised. He loathed the flippant manner and the open contempt for authority. Rogo was the tough kid who had crossed the line to join the forces of authority and conformity; like most converts, he was fanatical in his beliefs. But he had seen something else in this man that made him uncharacteristically anxious to find a compromise: a quality Rogo could not pin down. He recognized it by the instinct all police-men develop. A hundred times you step into a bar fight. Sometimes it's a Puerto Rican with an ax, sometimes a black with a knife, sometimes it's a bunch of Poles. It didn't matter. You took a quick look, and you knew you could take them, and batter them down with anvil fists.

Occasionally, not even once a year, you went through that door and saw a different type of man. It wasn't size, it wasn't toughness, it wasn't anything like that, but you always knew it. "Sure I coulda took him," he remembered hearing another cop say once, "but not without my .38 I couldn't." Here was another one. Rogo was not afraid. He was never afraid. But he was cautious.

He kept the gun on him. "So c'mon, mister. Let's hear it. Then mebbe we can talk some."

Jason shrugged. "That's got to stay my business, Batman."

The high steel hull of the ship amplified Rogo's roar to a thunderous boom, and it was not until the last echo had rung in the dark corners that they heard the splashing. Every head turned. A black head, arms, and shoulders appeared out of the small pool and swam to the side. The underwater diver heaved itself out of the water, tore off the mask, her hair tipping in torrents down her shining black back.

"I'm Hely," she said, and began to cry.

Fat ladies wear the finest jewelry. By the time they have found their potential source, have driven him on and up in the world, and have so subjugated him that every anniversary and birthday adds weight and worth to their fingers, necks, and wrists, they have also enjoyed at least thirty years good living. Incentive has gone, and their pride lies in the contents of wardrobes and jewelry cases rather than any steady reading of bathroom scales.

Fat women, also, are seldom fighters. When that flood gushed through the main dining room, it was the unadorned young who had fought for the surface, until they too sank back into the silence of their tinsel-draped tomb. The overweight and the old, decorated from their husbands' industry, lay beneath.

That was the philosophy by which Hely led her team of divers into the vast upturned cavern. It was easily found. She led them down the side of the sunken ship and, swinging on the inverted railings, along the deck and down the first steps. There as she wondered which way to go, she noticed the sign. She flipped her feet up in the air to read it. "Come and Say Hello to the New Year!" She followed the arrow past more steps and through the door.

The thirty-foot-high chamber had become a sealed bowl containing a carnage made even more hideous by the trappings of carnival. From what had been the floor hung the bolted-down tables. All the other contents of the room had been scrambled together when the ship' went over and the seas rushed in.

After the translucent blues of the clearer sea outside, Hely had to adjust her eyes to the cloudy gray of the water here. The only light seemed to come from the pale blue disks of the portholes, and from an oblong hatch in the far corner at the top of the room. With a wave of her arm she drew her stunned crew after her. She checked the depth gauge on the canvas strap around her wrist. They were well beyond the thirty-three-feet mark. They would have to decompress on the return. There was still no hesitation as she swam straight down into the sodden havoc.

She was right. The dead lay in mounds, dress shirts and billowing gowns their shrouds, and all around them were the foolish fripperies of good fellowship, the paper hats and streamers, waterlogged. The last few seconds of life had stripped them of standards of civilization which, even after centuries of acceptance, could never compete with the will to live. Men had trampled women. Young men had smashed aside older men. The dead were stacked in layers, according to their strength and determination. Hely smiled inside her mask: if these people, conformers and stalwarts all, could cast away the proprieties, what justification did she need?

She felt not the slightest distaste as she plunged into their bodies. They moved easily enough, weightless in the water. She grabbed a dinner-jacket collar from behind and pulled aside a young man, his hair still crisp and curly. She took a quick look at his watch: forty dollars, not worth taking. She rolled him away. Two more men, one with a disintegrating streamer round his neck, and a woman whose diamond-chip ring suggested true love and penury, merited no further attention. Hely was after the bad hearts, the asthmatics, the bronchitics, the obese and the self-indulged, the heavy smokers and hard liquor drinkers. They would have died first.

She found the first one under the Christmas tree. It must have been twenty-five feet high, and several bodies were trapped in its flattened branches now, almost as though they had been trying to climb it. Hely looked up. They must have been making for the hatch at the top of the room before the waters overtook them. When it had crashed over, some of the older guests had been caught. This one was a woman, hopelessly enmeshed in the silver branches of the tree. The light was poor, but through the murky gray of the water she caught the glint of gold. One-handed, she unclipped a bracelet. The woman's plump unsunned arm drifted down again. The worry that had marked her face with lines ·in life was still there in death. She had the dutiful look of the good wife. Hely pushed her out of the way. Her right hand was locked in that of a man. Her gray hair floated in absurd curls away from her head; her lipstick made a small brown wound of her mouth in the opaque light. Ten years of regular visits to the beauty salon had done nothing for the fat that folded persistently under her chin, and it was beneath those rolls that Hely saw what she wanted: a necklace of sapphires surrounded by diamonds. "My God," Hely mouthed. Her cold fingers struggled with the intricate catch. Three times her thumbnail slipped off the minute mechanism. The fourth time she slipped both hands around the woman's neck, gripped the clasp between finger and thumb of each hand and began to twist it. The swollen, stupid face swayed backwards and forwards as she worked as though caught in an undignified exercise. Finally, the clasp broke. Hely slipped it, together with the bracelet, into the rubber purse strapped to her belt.

To one side of the Christmas tree, a grand piano had overturned and trapped several bodies. Again, Hely swung aside the corpses of the young with their costume jewelry. Here she found an elderly woman. She must have been eighty at least. She looked oddly peaceful. She'd had more time to contemplate the grave, Hely thought. Hely pulled her hand out from beneath the piano. At last! This was the real thing. There were two rings, a beautiful square-cut emerald flanked with baguettes and a marquise-shaped diamond. Together they must be worth at least thirty thousand dollars. Hely drew the knife from her leg sheath. She tried to slash the fingers. She could not get enough momentum behind her hand on account of the drag of the water. She held the hand on the piano keyboard. The notes echoed feebly as she reversed her knife and used the serrated edge to saw through the fingers. Pretty gray-brown flowers mushroomed in the water. She held the fingers in one hand and tugged at the rings. The emerald was jammed under the swollen knuckle. Rings and finger went into her purse.

Buoyed by the water and freed from gravity, Hely worked away as weightless as a bird among the bodies. The weak light which caught the glitter of the tree and the colored decorations was enough to pick out the jewelry. After ten minutes, her purse was half full. The value, even on the black market she reckoned, must be over a hundred thousand dollars. A ghostly fish, incurious, watched as she wrenched a diamond flower-spray brooch off a proud bosom, and the victim's sodden paper hat, miraculously intact, slipped over open, unprotesting eyes.

Her work had disturbed the minor detritus, and the food and paper and cigars, together with the plaster from the walls, had become little more than sludge in the water. Through the clouds, Hely could just see the paddling shadows of her companions. Not one of them had dug down among the bodies as she had. They worked tentatively at the top and she could sense their disgust for the task. She felt a cold, hard anger inside. They were fine heroes lounging on the deck or the beach. That was all they were fit for, exhibits of mock masculinity for the admiration of tourist girls. When it came to real guts, they were limp-wrists. Hely had dreamed up this idea from the first Mayday call. She had planned it, had tempted and goaded them into it, had led them and told them what to do. Even then, they faltered and floundered for fear of dirtying their hands. She knew what would happen. When they got back to the *Naiad*, her haul would lie on the deck beside their timid collection of cheap garnet rings and ten-dollar brooches, and she would have to listen to their excuses and meet their weak, pleading faces. They had not the courage to defy her nor the courage to obey her. They looked like lions and acted like kittens. She would have to get rid of them.

When Hely saw the invaders come lancing through the gloom she knew their purpose at once. They swam in pairs. Hely watched their figures materialize. Two carried spear guns, the others held knives in their right hands, and they were making directly for the rummaging divers.

Hely settled herself gently on a heap of bodies, and pulled the nearest one on top of her. She felt it flop lightly against her and saw a smashed face close to hers. She grabbed his hair and pulled the head onto her shoulder so she could see. Above, Roland and the others were still daintily picking at the bodies when the invaders hit them.

It was like a slow-motion ballet in thick fog. The first two men, spear guns under their arms, back-paddled for a moment at about four yards distance. The *Naiad* divers worked on. Hely could not see the harpoon. She knew they had hit when two of her divers—one looked like the English boy—arched gracefully backwards and spun slowly in the water. The other invaders swept past. For a second, she could see the balance of the fight in their posture. The invaders were pointing down like arrows, preda-tory and aggressive, the *Naiad* divers were caught turning, turtle heads hunched into their shoulders, desperate arms extended to hold off the attackers. Then the figures, distinguishable only by their intent, merged. One, two, three, Hely counted the sudden clouds of bubbles that burst upwards. The invaders had slashed her men's regulators, and the compressed air which should have gone from the cylinder to their mouths was released into the water. Hely caught the glint of silver several times through the swirling waters. They were stabbing the drowning men.

The entire operation had taken barely a minute. The attackers regrouped in a soft-paddling circle and then broke up and began to swim around slowly. They were searching. Hely gripped the lapels of her silent escort and swung his body more directly above hers. His face rested on her mask. The color seemed to have been washed from his eyes and she stared into what looked like circles of soiled linen. A lustless arm rested on her breast. She moved her head a fraction for fear of being seen. Beyond his fronds of hair, she saw a black figure flat above her, propelling himself along with the occasional flick of his flippers. He circled, dipped down, and hovered by her. She realized her teeth were clamped hard on her mouthpiece. Surely he would see the bubbles? His progress had disturbed some of the bodies. Other bubbles rose, freed from their traps in the clothes and corpses. Hely gripped her boyfriend to her. The invader passed. She saw the black figures diminish and fade towards the top, and toppled the body off her.

The hatch. It was the only other way out. All the invaders might not have left the massive chamber, but at least they were out of sight. She flicked in and out of the piles of bodies, her flippers whipping urgently, her fingers pulling at the bodies beneath her, at hair and clothes and limbs, to speed her progress. Once she felt the cold meat of a hand in hers. A wet-suited corpse floated above her. She jerked the leg down and through the mask saw Roland's eyes. *In death as in life,* she thought, *weak and frightened.* She moved on, a shadow among shadows, frightened, but fixed in purpose. Next she was using the branches of the fallen Christmas tree to propel herself, and then she raced up the side of the wall and through the pale light oblong of the hatch. She looked behind: there was no sign of pursuit.

She thought about Roland and the boys. There was no cause for regret. They were worthless. It was almost as if they had contributed to their own deaths. She had had the guts to rummage deep into that graveyard, and had lived. They had not, and had died.

Her mind was quite cool. It focused only on survival. To survive the slums, she had learned how to duck, how to run, how to hide, how to lie, and how to smile. They had become reflex actions. Now Hely was running like a hare at the sound of a gun: quite instinctively. She fled as she had done many times before, thinking and planning as she moved. *Head for the stern*, she thought. That is out of the water and will give cover if those men are still around. She swirled along the corridors without a glance at the rooms she passed: a laundry, a library, a television room. She thrust past the soft-limbed bodies that were everywhere, using them as levers for speed. Hely sped through the passengers' quarters, onwards and upwards. She checked her depth gauge as she went. She must stop to decompress soon. Stopping was risky if the men were following, but to go on without decompressing from that depth was certain death. She twisted like an eel into a cabin.

Blue-and-white-checked bedcovers tangled on what had been the ceiling. A suitcase floated against the fitted carpet above her. The minutiae of someone's domestic life was shattered on the floor. An alarm clock, coffee cups, a glass still holding a twist of lemon, a ring. She picked it up and examined it. Cheap rubbish. She flicked it away in disgust. Suddenly, a face peered at her through the half-open door, and Hely snatched for the knife strapped to her leg. She relaxed with a sigh. The face, fixed in a bilious smile, floated slow and unwinking across the doorway. It was just another body, caught in some gentle current.

Hely thought. She had gone some distance towards the stern. Soon she would be under the engine room. Then she would surface and see if it was safe to return to the yacht. She still had her haul. The trip had not been entirely wasted. The gleaming green figures on her watch showed she had decompressed for seven minutes. It should be ample. She should be safe from the bends, that terrible flirtation with death that came from too rapid an ascent. She almost smiled as she remembered other chases in earlier days. It was always like this. Always in the dark. Then there had been the slam of a policeman's boots behind her, the skidding on corners, the swerving and the frantic grabbing for lungfuls of air. Then there was always the delicious moment when the pursuer was lost, the panting rest in the corner of an alley somewhere, and the chance to rejoice in the haul. Then it had been a snatched handbag perhaps. Hely patted her purse. She did not need to look this time. Life, she thought, never really changes. Only the stakes got bigger, and the policemen didn't wear boots anymore.

When she had seen the water beginning to brighten she knew she was nearing the surface. She headed for the light. It was not bright enough for the sky. It must be a pool somewhere in the boat. Then she had surfaced in the great dark barn and struggled to the side. There were some people. A little man with ginger hair. A girl. A man in an undershirt with a gun. She needed time to think. *Cry*, thought Hely, and the tears ran.

The story did not hang together. It offended all Rogo's instincts as a policeman. He reran it through his mind. A girl pops up in the middle of a sinking

ship looking like she'd just stepped out of the cen-
terfold of *Playboy*, unzips her rubber suit so's you
can see halfway to Kalamazoo, sobs like hell, gets all
the guys patting her back and wishing they were patting her ass, and then tells a story you wouldn't hand
a ten-year-old.

"Look, let's try to get it straight, lady," Rogo said.
He was kneeling down beside her, the gun still in
his hand. "You say you were on a cruise, you heard
the call, and you and your buddies came looking
for survivors. Okay. So where are your buddies? You
say they got trapped—where, for God's sake, and
how, and why couldn't you help them? You came
here—why not swim out the way you swam in and
go back to your boat? I'm not knocking your story
but there sure's one helluva lot of holes in it."

Rogo's questioning was not very popular with the
other men. Martin was on his knees, his arm around
the girl in enthusiastic consolation. "Don't worry," he
kept saying. "You're among friends now. We'll look
after you." He took her hand and squeezed it. His
little pink face shone with sincerity and excitement
too. James Martin, haberdasher, was still having the
adventure of a lifetime.

That was why he had returned. All his life he had
been nobody. His schooldays were spent in anxious
smiles to please the big guys. He was the last to be
picked for a ball game. Later he was the one the
girls kissed on the cheek and said was cute. Even
his business was the smallest in Anaheim. At the
Rotary meeting, Martin had to sit quietly and listen
to Delano who ran the big food store and old Marcus
Dowdney who owned the furniture business. Even
when he organized the Christmas raffle for them,

they hardly noticed him. "You did a great job there, Jack," Mr. Delano would say. Three years he had been a member, and he was so insignificant they didn't even know his name. James Martin despised himself a little, and his life a lot. He didn't want to go back home. And when he did, he wanted to have his photograph on the front page of the local paper. Boy, old Dowdney would know his name then.

For the first time in his life, he felt like a hero. He felt like a cowboy. He felt like a marine. He felt like all the things he had always wanted to be. James Martin, haberdasher, from Anaheim, the worst football player in high school, was on his knees in a sinking ship holding a beautiful woman in his arms. Anyway you looked at it, it beat selling socks.

He brushed her wet hair back from her face. "You'll feel okay in a few minutes. You just rest. Comfortable? My knee's not digging into you, is it?"

Hely's plight even dragged Manny Rosen out of his desperate longing to be away from this place. He sat on the girder beside her. "You listen to him, miss. He's right. You've had a nasty shock, I guess. You young kids nowadays, I don't know, you don't look after yourselves. Flesh and blood you are, you can only take so much." Belle had come out of that same pool and died. Her body was just a few feet behind him. She had been flesh and blood and now she was a lump of ice. "Listen to an old man," he added. "Take it easy, huh?" His hand wiped a smear of oil off his tragic, drooping moustache.

The girl was obviously distressed. Klaas agreed that the story was confused, but then the girl was shaken. "Coby," he whispered, "do you think I should go to the *Magt* and fetch the brandy? This young woman is badly shocked." He was a little surprised to see the hard set of his daughter's face. "I do not think she is in any danger of dying," she said. "She looks very much alive to me, papa." Coby had watched her every second since she climbed out of the pool. She had seen the imploring words and glances. She had seen the girl's wary look when Rogo said he was a policeman. She had seen something else in her eyes when she had looked at Jason, still leaning against the girder, his face unmoved. "I don't think she's quite as ill as she appears, father," said Coby.

Women's tears. Rogo had seen them before. No one had cried more than the seventeen-year-old girl who had strangled her mother with the belt off her coat, and then gone out and bought a new belt. He had seen innocent, beautiful faces before too. One of them had been on a photographic model who had left an ax in her boyfriend's head. Rogo was unimpressed by tears and beauty and innocence. He pressed his questions.

"Tell it again, lady, and a little more detail this time, please."

He felt Martin's furious look. "Don't you think you're being a little unfair, Mr. Rogo?" The question was as close to a challenge as Martin cared to go.

"Yes." This time it was Manny Rosen. His voice sounded censorious too. "Give the young lady a chance to recover first, then I'm sure she'll explain everything." He appealed to the whole group. "Anyway, we haven't time to go into all this now. Don't forget, we're sinking."

Sympathetic bystanders. Rogo knew all about them

too. He also knew how to handle them. "Thanks a lot for your tips, fellas, now how would it be if you just let me hear the lady talk?" He leaned forward to watch her face when she spoke. He was usually right about faces. "Let's have it again from the top. And slowly."

The girl closed her eyes and gasped. Manny and Martin exchanged looks. They had said all they dare.

She opened her eyes again. Rogo's questioning, remorseless gaze was still there. The lanterns yellowed the waiting faces. The red fires roared spasmodically. The slow dripping, like Rogo's questions, went on relentlessly. It was Jason's voice that cut in.

"Leave her, Rogo."

The cop did not move. "Shut up, cowboy," he replied. "I'll handle this."

"I told you, Rogo, she's had enough. Give her a break."

"And I told you, keep out of it." Rogo had turned now. He was rising, and the terrible struggle between the two men was being reborn. "Keep out of it, d'you hear?" He was almost shouting again.

This was it. The battle for supremacy, interrupted by Hely's arrival, established more fiercely than ever. It had to be settled. Jason had stopped lounging and teasing. He had moved away from the girder with his feet apart, and Rogo held the gun firmly on him. He was only a few feet away from Jason and he talked as he edged nearer.

"I've had enough, mister. I had enough of you the second I saw you. And if you don't like cops that's just too bad because . . ."

The girl's scream tore open the darkness of the vault. Rogo spun awkwardly, one foot raised on a chunk of metal, the other braced behind him. He had a quick flash of the girl in the wet suit with her mouth open. Then Jason hit him. Off balance, he crashed to the floor, twisting as he fell. Even as he landed he felt the gun torn from his hand and Jason's knee on his throat. "You goddamn sonofabitch!" The words came in a croak.

Manny started to tremble. Martin began to say, "I don't honestly think you're going to solve anything . . ." No one was listening. Martin finished the sentence weakly, for his own benefit, "by falling out like this."

Jason rose in one movement and backed three paces away. He kept the gun aimed at Rogo's stomach. He spoke evenly, without any hint of anger or excitement.

"You've got it all screwed up, Rogo. Maybe you've been on this boat too long. Maybe you shouldn't have come back. You're too jumpy. You're trying to hammer everyone into the ground. Forget what you think about me, and the girl too for that matter. We don't count. Think about your job. Remember, that's why you're here." Rogo's eyes flickered towards the hold. Uncertainty replaced the anger on his face. Jason was still talking. "This isn't a contest for who's the toughest kid on the block. There's half a billion dollars' worth of gold bars in there and you're supposed to be sitting on them for Uncle Sam. Remember! Old Glory, apple pie, all that crap you guys believe in. Well, believe in them. Do it! Do your job! You're a cop, Rogo. Act like a good one."

Coming slowly to his feet, Rogo wiped his hands on his thighs. "Okay, okay," he murmured. Louder, he said, "A guy asks a coupla questions and you go out of your tree."

It was over.

"And another thing," Jason said, but now he was grinning and the gun was swinging by his side. "This damned peashooter of yours. It's been soaked. Bet you a bar of gold you can't get a shot out of it." He pointed it into the black distance towards the propellers and squeezed the trigger steadily. It clicked harmlessly. "Bet you're glad you're not after Jesse James with that, Batman." He threw it across to Rogo, who caught it, looked at it, and sent it clattering among the wreckage by the small pool. It was only a lousy lady's gun anyway.

He said, "Yeah, well it don't really make so much difference. These days you gotta have an affidavit signed by Jesus Christ before you can pull the trigger. So what the hell! Come on then, cowboy, you're the one talking duty. Help me get that hold door open."

Side by side, the two men set off scrambling over the rubble.

"Whew, that sure was a relief." Hely hardly heard Martin's words. She had sat up to see the confrontation. Her own anxiety to shake off the pestering questions of the cop had gone. Her scream, she knew, had given the man in the old jeans the chance to move. But what a man. She had never seen anyone like him before. She had known strong men and tough fighting men, but this was different. He had talked the cop down. He had won the battle, and then calmly handed the gun back to the vanquished. Again the pink-faced man beside her was squeaking away, "Because if two guys don't hit it off together in this sort of situation . . ." Hely was not listening. She was thinking. That was the man. She must have that man. He was the one. She had seen what she wanted just as certainly and coldly as she had seen the rings on the fingers of the dead. She scrambled to her feet, holding down the excitement inside her.

"You seem to have recovered now." The young girl's comment was laced with disbelief. Hely was slightly amused. She was perfectly accustomed to women who did not like her. Presumably this little girl had her eyes on the American too. Hely delivered her most seraphic smile.

"How sweet of you to worry," she said. "I shouldn't have made such a fuss. I mean, it must be so much more frightening for a small girl like you." Shopgirls. They were all shopgirls to Hely. With their calf-eyed crushes and their mindless swooning and the bodies they hardly understood themselves. If the only competition around came from a schoolgirl in her first trainer bra, Hely could afford to be amused.

"Hey." Rogo's bellow came from the shadows. "How about bringing those lamps over here? I don't want this bum strangling me with his beads."

He's smart, thought Rogo, as they climbed towards the hold. *He's smart and he's tough, and he's straight, I think, but I still got to watch him.* Rogo hoped he would be on the level. If he wasn't, he could sure as hell cause a lot of trouble. He could hear the others coming up behind. At least Jason wasn't a cripple, that was something. Martin was explaining to that half-stripped blond all about Anaheim and the problems of the haberdashery trade. Rogo sighed, and promised himself he would volunteer for permanent traffic duty when he got back.

"C'mon there, snap it up," he called.

COMPANY

6

News of the *Poseidon*'s disaster commandeered the front pages of the world's newspapers, and thousands of politicians and film stars cursed to find their carefully scheduled publicity stunts driven out of the papers. A New York newspaper carried a photograph of Mike Rogo in which, as his friends remarked, he looked a good deal more criminal than anyone he had ever arrested. A young reporter from the *Anaheim Dealer* tried to get background information on Mr. James Martin, their newly minted local hero, only to discover that no one could remember what he looked like. A retired naval officer who had not seen water since 1945 found himself whipped from his rose garden

in Kent to the London television studios as an instant
expert on sea disasters. There was a great deal of
wild, fruitless speculation about what had caused a
New York cop to pull a gun on the rescue helicopter's
crew and insist on returning.

Television crews came up with dramatic footage of
the scene, and studio-bound reporters reconstructed
the events as they appeared on film. It was evident, they
all agreed, that the yacht *Naiad*, the *Magt*, and the
Komarevo were launching a salvage operation. The
retired naval officer pointed out the features on a
swiftly prepared mock-up of the cross section of a
cruise liner and explained how the *Poseidon* could stay
afloat. "It's rather like a giant sponge," he said, amazed
at his own knowledge. "Some of the cells are full of
water and are dragging it down, some remain full of
air and hold it up. The water must be advancing, and
as soon as the balance tilts, the ship will go down."
Exhausted, he retired to the hospitality room for a
pink gin.

He was substantially right. The *Poseidon* was held
in its position by dozens of pockets of air, some tiny,
some massive, that had been driven by the advancing
waters into the stern of the ship. The launderettes,
the car elevator, the garage, the indoor swimming
pool, and the Turkish baths, all inverted, held the
principal bubbles that kept the vessel afloat. Two
entire sections of the passenger cabins were free of
water. But the weight of the ship, bearing down on
the water, created an intolerable pressure that sooner
or later would burst the bubbles.

The retired naval officer, emboldened by forty
minutes in the hospitality room, told the nation at
the next newsbreak that it would happen slowly. One

by one the watertight doors and bulkheads would be broached, and the *Poseidon* would sink gracefully beneath the waves.

He was wrong. The garage and a whole section of cabins went simultaneously, and the water ripped through their silent rooms. This shifted the balance completely. The bow end became heavier and sank further, lifting the stern even higher out of the water.

The retired naval officer, dragged from the bar to consider the newly reported position for an emergency bulletin, took one look and said, "That's it. The next movement will be the last and the whole thing will go." This time he was right.

It launched another rash of spontaneous speculation. Would the rescue ships be able to do anything in time? How long could the *Poseidon* last? Why didn't the French navy send their helicopter back? The French navy replied courteously but firmly that they had already had one pilot almost shot and did not propose risking another.

A New York cop, over an afterwork beer with a colleague, offered the opinion, "If they think they can kill Rogo that easy they don't know the guy. You couldn't kill him with a napalm bomb." The reporter in Anaheim finally traced Mr. James Martin's mother, who, sobbing, told him, "All he ever wanted was to find a nice girl and settle down." He also found a photograph of him at a Christmas raffle; his face was obscured by someone's shoulder. Desperate relatives telephoned shipping line offices and newspapers. Cranks contacted radio stations with demented suggestions for saving the ship. A Portuguese zoo owner telephoned a newspaper to say he was worried about a Bengal tiger he had on board, on its way to Athens for a mating exercise. The reporter asked him if he realized that hundreds of people had died, and to hell with a goddamn tiger that would be dead anyway. The retired naval officer explained the factors that determined the Battle of Trafalgar; the producer wondered if he would last until the next bulletin. Mike Rogo's wife was described, charitably, by one newspaper as "an ex-show-biz girl." Mr. Manny Rosen's next door neighbor told her sister that Manny must have returned for his wife. "They were never apart, those two old lovebirds," she said. The New York cop considered his colleague's statement and replied, "The way that bastard Rogo rides everybody, I hope he's got lead in his boots."

The readjustment of the boat's position came as a heavy, rocking lurch to those inside. The alteration of angle, about three degrees, threw the wreckage of the engine room into a terrifying cacophony, and the two stinking pools, one similarly dark, the other still violently ablaze with hellish fires, drained suddenly. The waters vanished with a hideous gulping sound, and the flames died.

The seven people were flung against the bulkhead. Rogo twisted his arm around a chain across the front of the hold, and locked his other arm around Manny Rosen's waist. A wrecked catwalk came hurtling out of the darkness and crashed on the floor inches away from Klaas as he and Coby, hanging on to each other, skidded and toppled into a heap of bent handrails. Martin rolled over and over, landing on the Dutchman. Instinctively, Jason seized the girl in the wet suit, flung her against a girder, and locked powerful arms around it as the flying debris crashed and clattered about them.

The last echoes died. Three lanterns, mercifully unbroken, had also been thrown after Martin and the Dutch couple, and all three were illuminated in a crazy tangle, like some extraordinary floor show. Manny Rosen was sobbing. Rogo spoke to him gently as he released him, "It's okay, Manny. It's over now." It was what he called his New Widow's Voice, the one he used for bad news.

One by one, they disentangled themselves. Coby, surprisingly cool, helped her father to his feet. "You're very brave," Martin was saying to her, but she only nodded and saw that Jason and the fair-haired woman were still safe against the girder. The woman was a liar: she wished she could tell Jason.

Her arms around the American's waist, Hely felt her earlier excitement rise to a fine, high ecstasy. Her body sang with the frightening sexuality that for some people comes with the nearness of death. Storms of fear and courage and danger and fire engulfed her, and his body seemed to burn her where they touched. She turned her face up and tore a cannibal's kiss from his mouth. "I want you," she said, clear enough for the others to hear, and they watched in astonishment. "I want you, and I shall have you."

Jason leaned back to see her face. "You," he said, with measured words, "are one hell of a woman."

"Whaddya think this is, a stinking petting party?" Rogo reintroduced reality. "What in God's name is this tub doing?"

Klaas was holding his ribs where Martin had landed on him. He winced a little, and picked up his captain's cap and dusted it on his leg. "You'll have to be quick now, Mr. Rogo. That must have been the last major pocket of air to go. Next time she will go down."

In the wet soundless gloom, they all realized the import of his words. It had seemed hard to believe the *Poseidon* was sinking when it was so firm beneath their feet. Now they sensed the death throes of the old liner, and everyone knew the end could not be far away.

Slumping to the floor, Manny Rosen felt spent. Over where the pool had been, the waters had vanished and revealed the steps of the companionway. They led through into the boiler room and the corridors beyond that they had traversed in their flight for survival. That was where Belle had saved them all with her sacrificial underwater swim. Now Belle's body had gone. The lurch must have thrown it into the water, and it had been sucked away. It was as though the *Poseidon*, in its death throes, had claimed her. He had returned solely to bring Belle back and restore to her in death some of the fine pride she had in life. Now she had gone, swept away into the vast graveyard that lay beyond the engine room. Perhaps, thought Manny, this was how it was meant to be. He felt old and lonely and frightened now that he had lost his reason for being there. The bonds which had bound them together in life were now truly severed, and he was a man alone. He looked at the others and saw the grimness on Rogo's face. "Mr. Rogo," he said, in a low, steady voice. "Belle's gone now."

It went unheeded. Rogo, his face somber, asked Klaas, "How long? How long've we got?"

Klaas held out apologetic palms. "Who can say? Two hours, maybe less. The weight of the ship will pull down, eventually the last bulkheads will burst, and judging by the angle it will sink like a stone. We ought to be going, Mr. Rogo."

Two hours might be enough. Rogo's mind now was on his mission. "Okay, you guys, let's get this goddamn gold outta here and snap it up." He picked up a bar of shattered steel and began swinging it at the two chains which were padlocked discouragingly around the front of the hold door. The angry clang of steel on steel crashed around the room. Rogo's face lit up with furious energy. His eyes bulged and the sweat shone in the pale yellow of the lamps. One chain clattered to the floor. He hammered the second one like a blacksmith, and then, seeing one thick link begin to part, thrust the bar like a lever against the hold door. His shoulders strained. Ugly little grunts burst through his clamped teeth. His eyes rolled white. The chain gave suddenly, and Rogo barked with triumph as he crashed backwards into Klaas. "Right, fellas, let's get that gold and get the hell outta here!"

Klaas restrained him with one hand. "Not so fast, my friend. I am an old hand at carrying freight of all kinds. This hold could be flooded, or there could be fire in there. There could even be gas. We must proceed with caution. Does anyone know what other cargo was in the hold?"

His eyes were on Jason. He did not reply. Rogo said, "I dunno. I never saw inside. They just showed me where it was and said sit on it."

Another doubt had occurred to Klaas. "But a

fortune like that, and only these?" He kicked the dangling chains. "It hardly seems possible."

"That was the whole goddamn point." Rogo was pleased. For once, he was doing the explaining. "The stuff is packed in these Toledo Wire and Bolt cases. See? If they'd put shotgun guards and brand-new locks on it, someone mighta guessed. But no one was going to ask questions with just a coupla lousy chains."

"That's right." Jason was talking now. "I've got a . . . parcel in there. Put a nice innocent label on it and who's going to bother checking. Anyway, only the grease monkeys come down to the engine room."

The door had been the entrance to the top hold of three. Now, with the upturning of the ship, it was the lower one, and the bottom of the door almost met the ceiling-floor on which they were standing. The imperfectly stamped letters "HOLD NO. I" were upside down. Klaas pressed his hands and his ear against the flat authoritarian gray of the door. It was about seven feet high and four feet across.

"No fire, I think," he said, quietly, his hands testing the thick steel. "But I hear a noise. An odd noise. It sounds like an engine running and stopping, a sort of drumming. It could be water. I suggest we open it carefully." He indicated the ten six-inch handles around the edge of the door. "These fit into angled slots to hold it up against a waterproof pad. A little at a time with each, please."

Tentatively he edged one down an inch. Then the same with the next. Coby stepped to the other side. She too moved one handle a fraction, then another, then another. The rim of the door eased out very slightly. The only sound was their own breathing, and a muffled rasping noise that grew louder as the door came away from its pad. It was familiar and yet also unidentifiable. Rogo and Jason exchanged baffled looks.

"Any minute now, gentlemen," murmured Klaas. He tapped each of the handles lightly so that they lost their final, fractional grip. "Any minute . . ." In that second of bright fear, a terrible roar seemed to engulf the whole engine room and shake the ship itself. In a gap an inch wide they saw beyond belief and all doubt the ferocious beauty of a tiger's face.

For a second that might have been an hour, time ended, and it seemed as though their senses had surrendered to havoc. All of them froze at the madness of what their eyes told them. The rich colors of that great head, the thick curving black lines sharply delineated against the orange yellow, blazed in the light of the lanterns. It was a picture of beauty and terror, framed perfectly between door and frame. Coby, frozen in a stooping position where she had been loosening the last handle, looked straight into the tiger's eyes. She felt as though she were looking beyond the end of the world. The terror of that timeless moment was suspended, for the animal's head was cocked slightly to one side in a puzzled, almost inquisitive way, like a dog who thinks he hears his name. From Rogo issued an involuntary "Sheeeyit!"

Then the tiger's face divided like a chasm and all sensations exploded in a vision of cavernous mouth and teeth and again a roar waved and rolled across them, a tempest of noise and power that seemed to scorch the flesh and crack the bones. And around the edge of the gradually opening door, a huge paw appeared. At first blindly, touching and feeling, and then clamping down on Coby's left arm.

Rogo, immediately behind her, swayed, and sank to his knees, his knuckles on the ground. He was powerless. Klaas, beside the girl, was quite immobile, his fingers locked around one of the handles, and Manny Rosen's jaw swung in a caricature of dislocated astonishment. It was Martin who moved and spoke first. He almost jumped in the air and babbled, "Quick, do something!"

Jason swung Hely to one side. He raised himself up on his toes, took seven or eight, finely balanced steps, then his foot lashed out in a perfectly judged, curving kick that landed in the center of that paw. From the embers of the roar blazed another, this time a sharper, more sudden sound, and the paw flicked back out of sight.

"Everyone!" yelled Jason, and flung himself at the hold door. Coby threw her weight with his, and Klaas, awakened by Jason's action, joined them. Jason snapped two of the handles back into the locked position, and gave a gasp of relief. He leaned back against the hold. Coby took his hand and looked at her sleeve. It was ripped. "Thank you" was all she could manage.

"Never, never in my goddamn life have I seen anything like that." Rogo was shaking his head from side to side in long, slow turns. He was talking to himself. He held out his hands, palms down, and examined them. They were twitching, and his chest rose and fell too quickly. "You know, I don't think I was ever really scared before, not in my whole life."

Manny put a hand on his shoulders. "We were all the same, Mr. Rogo. Don't you worry about it. Except for Captain Jason there. It's a good thing he jumped pretty quick or the young lady could have been in real trouble."

Rogo knelt there looking at his shaking hands and thinking. It shouldn't have been like that. He had faced most dangers. He had been shot, he had been knifed, he had been beaten up. Four men had cornered him once behind a liquor store they were sticking up on Ninety-seventh Street. He had accepted that fear then, and advanced to meet them, knowing he could be killed. Two weeks in the hospital that time, and his nose would never be straight again. Then there was the Westchester Plains prison mutiny. He had walked in, shot three armed criminals, and put an end to a riot. Again at the risk of his life. He was not stupid; he had known that when he did it. But the apprehension he felt then was nothing like this. "Holy suffering Christ!" he murmured. "A big pussycat did this to Mike Rogo." He was glad Linda had not been there to see it.

"We were all pretty shocked, I guess," Martin said. "I mean, a tiger. Well who'd expect to find a tiger in there? Don't let it worry you. I was scared myself, Mr. Rogo."

It was the comparison that did it. The thought that Martin dare set his courage and toughness alongside his own brought Rogo growling to his feet and flexing his fingers. "That's okay for you. I bet you stand on a chair if you see a mouse. But Mike Rogo don't scare, period. And he don't like it when he does, either."

"I was only trying to help." Martin bristled. Rogo was always picking on him. He had done as much as anyone in the first escape. And he had volunteered to come back. "At least I could still talk and didn't just sit there."

"Talk! Yeah, that's about the only stinking thing

you're good at," Rogo snapped back. "And I'll tell you something, Martin. One of these days you're gonna wind up picking your teeth up offa the floor if you don't quit yapping. I wanted a tame canary, I woulda brought one."

His arm still around Coby, Jason heard the little Dutch girl whisper, "Oh, please stop them!" Jason's tone was back to its customary light banter when he spoke. "Any other time, gentlemen, and I'd be glad to hold your jackets, but unfortunately we've got work to do. What I'd like to know is what the hell a tiger's doing in a passenger ship's hold anyway."

Klaas explained, "Cargo, that's all. This is no longer the gracious queen of the seas it was once, you know. I'd say that they'd carry anything and everything to make the voyage pay. Greek shipowners are not sentimentalists."

Coby said, "Yes, but a tiger, Papa?"

Klaas shrugged. "Someone must transport them. This hold had a little more security than most, so I suppose they thought it would be safer in there. Probably did not even feed the beast. From what I hear, the *Poseidon*'s new owners are not too choosy about their cargo as long as the money is right." Jason gave him a thoughtful look. "They sure don't ask too many questions, Klaas."

Klaas continued, "That doesn't matter. What does matter is that we can't get in there anymore. This ship can go down any minute. The situation is hopeless, and I suggest we abandon ideas of salvage of any sort and get back to the *Magt*."

Manny Rosen could not agree quickly enough. "There's nothing we can do here anymore. We tried, but I think we ought to face facts and get out quickly." He shuddered slightly as he looked around the hostile darkness.

Rogo obviously did not agree. His fists sat truculently on his hips. "You hit a coupla snags and you run away. But Mike Rogo stays, tiger or no goddamn tiger."

Hands outflung in despair, Klaas made one last appeal to him. "But you cannot recover the gold. It's impossible." Rogo found it hard to argue with Klaas. His quiet authority, his knowledge of the sea, his captain's insignia, the very reasonableness of his manner. Perhaps it was impossible. Perhaps he would be risking his life for nothing. Every instinct told him he must recover that consignment. But he knew in his heart he could never steel himself to open the door and face that creature again. He found himself turning to Jason, "You got any ideas, cowboy?"

It was as near as the New York policeman could get to a plea, and Jason responded as best he could. He was examining the hold door, his thumbs hooked into his jeans' pockets, and he said, "You're right, Rogo. I'm in the same position. I still want to collect my . . . parcel, but I don't particularly want to play Tarzan with that cat. The ship's going to go down soon. And any minute now we could have company."

The last sentence made everyone look at him.

"Company?" Rogo glared. "Company? We're in the middle of the lousy, stinking sea, not Fifth Avenue, dumbo."

Only Hely was not completely stupefied by the comment. She thought of the men who had attacked her and killed Roland and the others. Jason must know them. They knew of her mission certainly, and she suddenly realized that she might be exposed. What would Jason think of her then? She said quickly, "I think we'd better go, Jason, before it's too late."

They all watched as Jason turned and indicated with a casual finger the far side of the vessel, between the stern and the pale light of the recently revealed companionway. "I'm afraid it is too late," he said.

On the blackness of the hull's side, a thin, fiery red line had completed three sides of a square, and there was a clear hissing sound. Rogo, who only an hour earlier had rejoiced at the same operation when he was rescued from the propeller shaft housing, knew instantly what it was.

"They're cutting through," he said. He creased his brow over this new mystery. How the hell would Jason know someone was coming? Were these some friends of his? His doubts about the man swept aside the mild comradeship that had developed between them. Rogo's eyes narrowed and he wished fervently he had his gun, in working order.

He growled aggressively at him, "Okay, this time no party games, huh? Who is it out there? What's going on? This ain't funny no more."

"No," replied Jason, and his amiable tone did nothing to lessen the shock of his words. "I think it's going to get very unfunny from now on. Our new guest, if I'm right, is Captain Ilich Bela, and, whatever else he does, he does not make people laugh. He is a Communist. He is also a smuggler, a blackmailer, a thief, and a murderer. He is the leader of a band of thugs who'd make your clients, Rogo, look like Shirley Temple."

Rogo was stunned. He asked quietly, "What does he want here?"

Jason tossed a thumb at the hold door. "Gold. Wherever there is gold, Captain Bela won't be far away. And if you want to go back on your beat with two legs, don't stand in his way, Batman."

The hissing red line was halfway along the fourth line of the approximately six-foot square in the side of the hull, its base just above the waterline outside, with a ten-foot drop to the wreck-strewn floor of the engine room. Its progress held all their eyes. There was no conviction in Rogo's voice as he grunted, "Well, I ain't giving ground to a Commie pirate bastard."

"Captain Jason, I feel sure that if we explain . . ." Klaas began, but he stopped when he saw Jason's head shake.

"Ilich Bela isn't the debating type, Klaas. He does most of his talking with bullets."

The hissing stopped. The square was completed.

It was going to be a good day. It was, thought Anton happily, going to be a very good day. He sat in the stern of the eight-seater pinnace watching the men working with the cutting gear on the hull of the *Poseidon*, among showers of golden sparks. He hummed a popular song quite tunelessly. Soon he would have fun. Lots of fun. He would have money. Then he would buy girls and vodka. A smile of almost cherubic innocence rested incongruously on his ape face. Anton's pleasures were simple. They were violence and vodka and women, and all three were soon to be delivered to him.

"Soon, eh, Captain Bela?" The captain, in front of him, nodded and smiled over his shoulder. Then he leaned back and snapped disagreeably as some of the sparks drifted dangerously near his jacket. A curious man, Captain Bela. So fond of his clothes. Like a woman almost, with his manicured hands and soft voice, thought Anton. But that was only the captain's way, like his strange manner of talking. Anton liked him, loved him almost. Captain Bela was a good man. He was not afraid of anyone, despite the softness in his hands and voice. He knew how to get money, and he knew how to keep away the police. Anton did not like the police. But since he had become the captain's friend he had not been to prison once. And what had the captain told him that morning? "Anton, my friend, how would you like a policeman to play with?" Anton had been puzzled at first. The captain had explained with his clever, confusing words, "To play with, Anton. A little policeman for you to play with. He is on that ship and he must not leave alive. Do you understand?" Anton had understood then. There had been other people the captain had not wanted alive, and always it had meant fun for Anton. The captain had said there was gold on the ship too, and Anton could have some for his girls and his vodka.

His hand rooted for an itch in his coarsely matted chest. He was contented. He hoped he would not have to use the pistol in his belt. It was too much like a little toy. Too quick, too sudden. Anton wanted to use his hands. He looked at them. The great pads of muscle under each finger. He had once strangled a dog with his left hand for a bet. It was a big dog and it had kicked and wriggled as he held it out at arm's length. But it had been easy, as he felt his fingers clamp on that hot throat. Anton had enjoyed that feeling more than the small vodka he had won.

Perhaps the policeman would kick and wriggle too. That would be good.

The sparks stopped. The men had finished cutting. The metal cooled quickly. One of them leaned back and banged the sole of his boot against it. Quite slowly, the great square of steel fell in, landing somewhere inside with a hollow crash.

"Let's find some little games for you, eh, Anton, my friend?" The captain had risen. He straightened his cap and made a small adjustment to his lapel, and then, motioning with the heavy-caliber automatic pistol in his hand, directed Anton and three others to the front. Anton grabbed the rope ladder and put it under his arm, and shouted, "Me first!" He stepped up onto the rim of the opening. It was going to be a good day.

OPEN THE CAGE

7

They had faced many dangers. Rogo and the other two original survivors had conquered the grueling climb through the inverted ship, and returned. All of them had experienced the sudden terror of the ship's lurch, the nagging ever-present dread that at any moment it would sink and take them with it, and the jarring shock of the tiger. They had been in fear, sometimes of each other even, in the dripping darkness of that dreadful floating coffin. The arrival of Captain Bela, however, was a new dimension in danger. They watched his boarding party in fearful silence.

From the moment the cutaway section of the hull crashed inwards, they were aware of the malevolent nature of the intrusion. Pearl light flooded the forward end of the room, the now water-free companionway to the rest of the vessel, the wreckage of machinery across what had originally been the ceiling, and on the far side the little group who stood in front of the hold. They blinked at the neat square of blue sky as the rope ladder snaked over the side. There was no cheerful inquiry, no offer of assistance, no identification, none of the signs that would have indicated honest men in a rescue operation. And no hope could have survived the sight of the silhouetted giant who for a second completely blocked the new source of light, and then swung silently down the ladder.

Manny, who stood with Martin and Klaas and his daughter near the hold, whispered, "He looks like King Kong."

Rogo had advanced to meet the new arrivals. He thrust out his rock face, prepared to take on all comers, a few feet away from the foot of the rope ladder. But there was little confidence left in him, and the lumbering giant ignored his challenge: "What do you think this is—Visitor's Day?"

Three more men followed, each in what appeared to be a uniform of turtle-necked maroon sweaters and knitted woolen hats. The first, they saw, had only one eye. It made him look even more sinister. Another mean-faced one fingered his growing moustache with a novice's pride. They moved without speaking, two to the right by the drained lake which led down to the funnel, and two to the left near the companionway. Each man carried a Russian Stechkin automatic pistol. The guns were trained on the group throughout the boarding operation and when they took up their positions their regimentation suggested a firing squad.

There was something close to admiration in Rogo when he said, "Jesus Christ, Jason, these guys are no amateurs."

Jason's reply came, surprisingly, from some distance away. He was behind Rogo. "Don't worry, Batman," he said. "They know their job. Let me take care of this, Rogo, huh?"

Rogo grunted assent. There was little else he could do. He recognized professional killers when he saw them. He himself was no longer armed. At least Jason appeared to know who they were. But why had Jason moved so that he was alone? It was as though he had detached himself from the group. Rogo didn't like it.

Grim-faced, Klaas watched their arrival. The sea, like the land, has its own levels of society, and Klaas was under no illusion about these men. No ship's crew he had ever seen behaved like this. They were gangsters beyond doubt. They were not the shabby crooks and petty thieves of dockland either; they were trained, ordered, practiced. His arm went round his daughter, and he felt her shiver against his chest. She, too, knew.

Martin, for perhaps the first time, began to wonder if the adventure was worth the risk. There was no ignoring these men or misjudging their character.

They felt as though they were watching the erection of their own gallows. When a slim, poised figure appeared in the blue square, it was without doubt the entrance of the hangman.

"Now, gentlemen," he said, "let us see what fish

we have caught." His excellent English was made even more sinister by the softened consonants of Eastern Europe. He descended the ladder, taking care to see it did not touch his clothes, and as he stepped to the floor he half-snapped his fingers in irritation at some smear of dirt. As he faced them, the powerful beam of his flashlight lit the barrel of a gun in his right hand.

Rogo was caught like the principal actor in the floodlight, screwing his pugnacious face against the glare. Behind him, it showed Martin and Manny standing together, Klaas holding his daughter, and the wet-suited girl tall and straight and unflinching.

The beam lifted to catch Hely more directly. "Ah yes, of course. The one that got away. I believe you met some of my colleagues earlier." She did not reply. Rogo thought for a second of all his unanswered questions. To one side, Jason raised a puzzled eyebrow for his benefit alone.

The silky voice went on with its commentary as the flashlight continued its search of the room. "Here, I presume, we have the captain of the little freighter." Klaas gave a formal, stiff bow. "A girl, two little men whose New Year's Eve dinner must have been rudely interrupted, and a tough guy." The last remark came as the light landed again on Rogo's narrow-eyed face.

"Ladies and gentlemen," the voice soothed, with elaborate courtesy. "May I introduce myself. I am Captain Ilich Bela, captain of the salvage ship *Komarevo*, and I am afraid that from now on you must accept that I am in authority here."

The eloquent beam momentarily illuminated the armed guards on either side.

"I am, in this context, a salvage expert."

Another voice, equally casual, cut in. "An expert in salvaging other people's money, an expert in smuggling and stealing and killing. Right, captain?"

It was Jason. Bela's swiftly moving beam found him sitting astride a shattered generator, his back against a girder. He was grinning. "Well, Bela," he went on, "I had a feeling you might be dropping in."

His smile held through an interminable silence. At last, Bela spoke, "You have the advantage of me, Jason. What are you doing here?" He was obviously shocked, and not too pleased.

Jason grinned back, "Why, the same as you, of course. Trying to earn an honest crust."

The light again flashed on the expressionless figures of the three gunmen and the towering Anton, and Bela's words came clipped and anxious, "Don't play games with me, Jason. You should know better than to try to take me lightly."

Mock gravity replaced the grin. "Don't try to frighten me with your trained poodles, Bela."

Rogo was confused. He did not like the familiarity between the two of them. What was so special about Jason that he could joke with this crew of killers? He demanded, "What the hell is going on here?"

Jason explained, "Bela is quite a character. He's probably the only Communist ever to grasp the principle of the profit motive. But he also knows his limitations. And he knows that if he kills me, there isn't a port anywhere he could land and stay alive for twenty-four hours. Isn't that a fact, Bela?"

Bela sounded more composed again. "You have a lot of friends, Captain Jason. But why argue? We are in the same line of business."

"Oh no we are not!" Jason's gravity was quite genuine now.

Bela was teasing. "Come, Jason, you surprise me. I heard your name mentioned in connection with several rather unorthodox cargoes."

The others watched this meaningless exchange in silence. Jason spoke quite evenly. "My business is my business, Bela. But I don't make money out of arming murderers. I don't take checks for slitting throats. I don't shift Mafia men across frontiers. No, Bela, we're not in the same business at all."

"Ethics, my dear Jason, mere ethics. We both supply demands. It is the law of your admirable capitalist world, is it not? I may do it for money, you may do it for some more romantic motive. It is the same thing."

The discussion halted as one of the half-lit figures moved forward. The guns and lights turned on him. It was Klaas. He looked what he was, frightened but determined.

There was a slight quaver in his voice as he gripped tightly onto a bent rail and said, "Captain, I wish to speak with you. I have a line aboard this vessel, and you must realize that you are trespassing and will be held to account for it. As captain of the authorized salvage operation, I am in charge and I must ask you to withdraw and take these armed men with you."

Bela's laugh was full of enjoyment. Anton, bored with the talk, grunted with pleasure. He did not understand. But if Captain Bela was laughing then everything was all right.

"Skip it, Klaas." The Dutchman heard Jason's plea. "Keep out of this."

"No, no," said Bela, still burbling with laughter. "The good captain is right. We must address ourselves to the facts of the situation. And, of course, my good fellow, you do have salvage rights. That is a fact. It is also a fact that I can, if I wish, kill you and all your companions. You will still be quite within your rights. I shall see to it personally that it is inscribed on your gravestone."

The Dutchman's face crumpled. The order by which he lived had no application here. He was a man of peace among men of violence. He was powerless. He backed slowly out of the light.

"Now let us come to another fact," Bela continued. "Which of you is Detective Lieutenant Michael Rogo?" Silence. He gestured impatiently with the flashlight. "Come now, which one?"

No one looked at Rogo. The cop stood where he was. He was amazed when he heard Martin's shaky voice say, "Me, I'm Mike Rogo." They all looked, everyone incredulous. "I'm the cop," he added, and folded his arms in an unconvincing gesture of masculinity.

It was his big chance. He had watched with envy as Jason and Rogo had led the action and made the decisions. No one ever asked him what he thought. Now he was up there with the men, even if he was frightened. He knew that he could be committing suicide.

The response he got was not what he expected. Again Bela's clear, amused, and pleasant laugh rang out. Whatever Captain Bela's weaknesses, he was an authority on policemen. He knew, for instance, that they did not come five foot six inches high with freckled faces and voices like choirboys.

"Ah, a little hero, I see. Very brave, my friend, but it will not do, I am afraid. I would say that the policeman must be our silent friend here." His gun barrel in the light indicated Rogo. "Yes, he has the right look of cretinous hostility."

Rogo kept his eyes on the gun. He said, "So I'm Rogo. What's it to you, pal?"

Bela had reverted to his persuasive mood again. "There you are, Anton," he called across. "I promised you a little fun."

Anton lurched forward, delight all over his face.

"Tame gorilla, huh?" Rogo said. "Call him off, fella, or I might have to throw him back in the trees."

Play it the way you know best, Rogo told himself. *Don't back off before hired muscle.*

Bela was talking again, "You see, Lieutenant Rogo, you set us something of a problem. I personally, of course, have no argument with you. However, my employers feel it would be better if you did not leave this ship."

The tone, the setup, the type were all familiar to Rogo. What he did not understand was the background to all this. "Why me?" he asked.

"Those are my instructions," Bela sighed, with infinite regret. "My employers are anxious that the world shall not know about your cargo of gold. You are surprised I know about it? Ah, officer, the world is perhaps a good deal more complicated than you realize. Now please tell me where it is stored."

So this guy was just a hood who wanted the gold. He might shoot him. But at least now Rogo would know why. He stabbed out a finger at Bela.

"This lousy tub must be about a hundred miles long and most of it's under water. So you go swim for the gold, wise guy, because I ain't telling." He clamped his arms across his chest. Rogo was going down fighting.

Bela was angry. He was totally conscious of the time limit set by the boat's precarious position. He issued rapid instructions:

"Get those sheep lined up over there. I do not want people hiding in corners."

Directed by the gun barrels, Manny and Martin, Klaas and Coby and lastly Hely moved along the bulkhead into the light, where they grouped blinking by the companionway. Jason did not move. He stayed in the shadows, a few feet in front of the hold door. Bela ignored him.

When he turned again to Rogo, Bela was sharp and businesslike. "You will tell me where the gold is and you will tell me quickly. I am not prepared to be hindered by some ignorant American policeman."

Rogo stepped closer to him and no fear showed. "And I ain't going to cooperate with a fancy-talking smart-ass Commie."

Bela was decisive and explicit. "Anton—break his bones!"

A look of anticipatory pleasure covered Anton's face.

Rogo braced himself as he heard the giant lumber up behind him. He felt his own steeled biceps squash beneath fingers of terrible strength. He closed down the shutters of his mind and surrendered himself to the future.

It was several seconds before he realized that the calm drawl he heard was Jason talking.

"If you want to waste time bashing cops, Bela, go ahead," he was saying. "But I would have thought a guy like you would be more interested in a deal. This ship is sinking, you know."

"What deal?" All playfulness was gone from Bela.

"Rogo knows and won't tell. You unleash the gorilla on him, it wastes time and you haven't got a lot of that left. Besides, Rogo might not talk for a long time. Look at him. He's all leather, that guy."

Bela was impatient. "What deal?"

Jason still flopped unconcerned against the girder. He said, "Me, I'm in the neutral corner here. I'm not on anyone's team. And I know where the gold is too."

They were going to kill Mr. Rogo. Manny could see that quite clearly, and he marveled at his own lack of horror at the situation. It seemed as though he could not feel anything anymore. The sequence of disaster and tragedy and menace had anesthetized him. He was numb. He trudged on mechanically. All the talk of gold, the tiger, even these evil men with guns did not seem to touch him. He watched it all wonderingly. Rogo appeared to understand it. So did Jason. Even little Martin wanted to be a part of it. But Manny felt himself to be a spectator at a grotesque charade: he had no role. Now they were going to kill Mr. Rogo and he could not understand why Rogo did not protest.

His eyes returned to the steps of the companionway, barely four feet away. He leaned back against the bulkhead, and could feel the tension and fear of the others beside him, feeling nothing himself. He could see the steps that led through to the rest of the ship, to that terrible journey they had made. Belle had died there. That too was where her body had been swept by the merciful waters; plucked from his sight. He refocused on the tangle of debris on the floor. The light had improved since these men had cut a hole in the side of the ship. He could see the pipes and conduits now. Of course, he remembered, that had been the ceiling. The ship was upside down. Everything was upside down. Throwing his mind back to the time before everything was upside down was as difficult as recalling childhood. Scenes before the catastrophe flashed back to him, like old photographs. Belle tidying her cabin. "It's our home, Manny, at least for a little time." The New Year's Eve celebrations that terrible night. With a start he realized it had only been the night before. It could not be possible. But that was when his world had, in every sense, turned upside down, and there was a memento of that time down there amongst the rubble. It was a champagne bottle. It must have been part of that New Year's Eve celebration, swept through the ship on the rising waters, and then stranded as the lurch altered the angle of the liner.

Then he saw something else beside the bottle. It was jammed between two of the conduits, and it took him a full minute to recognize it among the flotsam and jetsam of metal and machinery. Rogo's gun. Manny had seen hardly half a dozen in his life. He knew plenty of people who kept firearms. Self-defense they called it. But Manny never wanted to play around with them. "Dangerous," Belle always said, and he agreed. Anyway, who'd want to hurt poor old Manny Rosen? The day Manny joins the Cosa Nostra, he gets a gun. Belle used to laugh at that. What was Rogo's gun doing there? Ah yes. He remembered. Rogo had thrown it away when he discovered it didn't work. No one wants a pistol that doesn't work. Obvious, thought Manny, even to me who knows nothing about guns.

Through the insulation of shock that had protected him from the madness around him came a message so clear he almost jumped. His eyes riveted on the gun. It was such a small one, not a bit like the big pistols policemen usually carried. It had been soaked. But, and he grabbed the fleeting thought, these men did not know it would not fire. As the aged force their legs to carry them, Manny Rosen began to force his tired, stunned mind to work on that thought. He knew what he must do, and he knew too that he could do it. Belle would have wanted it that way.

It all rested between Bela and Jason now. The hovering violence, the threat of the looming Anton, the gritted courage of Rogo, faded. The tension between these two men was as taut as a wire from one side of the hull to the other. Bela dropped his elaborate courtesy. Jason abandoned his idle teasing. They were talking business.

Bela saw the opening that Jason was offering. "You will tell me?" he asked. He instinctively looked for the catches.

"For a price, Bela. And you know all about the price of things."

Bela nodded. "What price?"

They were trading now. Jason said, "I have a consignment in the same place. I take my parcel, you take your gold. That is the deal."

The silence in the engine room was agonizing as Bela thought. He spoke slowly. "That is possible, Captain Jason. You and I could reach an understanding. If we can perhaps help each other and make life a little easier, why not? On the other hand, what happens to our friends here? You see, it is part of my business that the policeman must not leave alive. It is essential. I have guaranteed it."

Rogo listened as his life was bartered. Anton was simply holding him, waiting for Bela's word to start.

Jason's fingers drummed the girder behind his back. His face did not move. He said simply, "So who'd miss a cop anyway?" And Bela smiled.

Martin, Klaas, and Coby flinched at the way Jason threw away Rogo's life. Manny seemed not to hear, his eyes rooted to the floor. Hely showed no emotion of any kind. But she kept her gaze on Jason, watching and wondering: there had to be something else, she thought.

Rogo half-twisted in Anton's grip. "Now hold it a minute! I don't care who's holding the goddamn guns, no one makes a deal with my life until I get something to say about it." No one looked at him.

Coby's sobbing followed his roar. "Please, please, please, Captain Jason, don't say that!"

Bela and Jason continued to regard each other as though there had been no interruptions. "One moment." Bela sounded a little curious. "How can you be so sure I will let you walk out of here with your parcel? It can hardly be, Jason, that you have such a high regard of me that you would take my word."

He was still looking for the trap. Jason gave a short bark of a laugh. "No, Bela, I wouldn't trust you with the church funds. I can walk out of here for the same reason I am safe now. You can't kill me, Bela. You don't want that much trouble. You know my friends, and you know they'd find you."

"You're right, of course," Bela said, pleased and a little relieved. "We are in permanent checkmate, you and I, Jason. So I will buy your deal and we shall both profit from it."

Hely still searched for the explanation. Bela, she

was sure, was every bit as merciless and murderous as he appeared. His part of the deal was straight-forward. But Jason? No. It was wrong. He operated by motives she could not begin to guess, but she knew this could not be as it appeared: the whole scene was false to her. There was not even a flicker on his face as he turned to her and said, "Okay, Hely, open up the hold and show the captain here his surprise."

It was all she could do to suppress the laugh. The tiger! So that was it. They had all forgotten it, except Jason. That was the surprise. And Jason knew that the tiger's arrival would give him an advantage, a chance to strike. She ducked under the piping and scrambled over the wreckage, and it was only when she reached the hold door that she appreciated exactly what it meant.

When she opened the door, she could swing it back so that she would be protected. Manny and the others were across the engine room and would at least have a chance to scramble to safety. But Jason was only a few feet in front of the hold, directly in the tiger's path.

She looked at him and saw in the grimness of his face that he knew exactly what he was doing. He understood her doubt, and his response too was unequivocal.

"Go ahead, Hely. Open the cage."

"YOU'RE A KILLER, MANNY"

8

There should not have been a hold there at all, but Bela was not particularly surprised. It was rumored in the shipping world that the *Poseidon*'s new Greek owners were so anxious to make the old queen of the seas show a profit that they were mixing freight and passengers, dropping the old five-star standards regardless of reputation, and that they would carry just about anything anywhere. The hold must originally have been some sort of storage space, but, like everything else on the old liner, it had been made to pay its way.

The door opened without a creak on well-oiled hinges. Hely's hand knocked down the securing handles

and swung the door completely around so that she
was obscured by it. Nothing happened. No one spoke,
no one moved. Everyone's eyes were riveted to that
black hollow. Inside, dimly visible, were piles of packing cases, some smashed. Bela started towards it, saying, "Well, let us take a look . . ." when the tiger
bulleted out.

It came from behind the cases. It moved at a fast,
low run, as though its stomach were touching the
ground, and it hurtled over the obstacle course of
the floor quite soundlessly. Jason had turned sideways
and pressed himself against the steel upright. It was
only about six inches wide and the hot, heavy body
of the beast brushed hard against his legs as it tore
past. His rigid body swayed from the impact and for
a second he closed his eyes. But he did not move.

The tiger stopped suddenly. It was frightened and
hungry. When the ship had turned turtle its cage had
been smashed, and since then the tiger had been flung
about in the darkness of the hold with the packing
cases at every new lurch and shift of position. Its
great head turned to take in its new surroundings. It
was halfway between Jason and Bela, some feet to
the left of where Anton held Rogo. It rose on its
hind legs, dropped its front paws gracefully onto an
oil drum, flung back its head, and roared.

The effect was immediate. The one-eyed gunman
standing in the debris towards the stern fell over backwards as though he had been struck. He lost his gun
and without a thought for it began scrambling on his
hands and knees up the mound of broken machinery
behind him. Bela spun like a dancer and launched
himself in a long, agile leap for the rope ladder. Of
the two men near the companionway, the one with

the thin moustache rocked back against the ship's side, his gun loose in his hands, and made a low moaning noise; he was quite helpless. The other man dropped to one knee, lifting the metal-framed stock to his shoulder, and ripped off a burst at the tiger's side. He emptied the full clip of twenty bullets with one squeeze of the trigger. The tiger snarled and twisted under the impact. Then it leapt. It passed Anton and Rogo in two gigantic bounds, and seized the kneeling man by the shoulder. His weapon clattered to the floor. His right arm flapped in futile protest at the tiger's head. For a second, the beast paused and stared again around the room, the man held loosely in its mouth like a half-chewed bone. Then, like a stoned cat, it bounded down the companionway and out of sight.

Now was the chance for the movements Rogo had been rehearsing in his mind. He saw Bela swinging out of control on the rope ladder; one gunman still scrambling up the heap of metal, blinded by fear; the other slumped against the side, groaning and sobbing.

Rogo went into a well-practiced routine. He stamped down hard with his heel on Anton's toe. He pumped his elbow viciously backwards into Anton's stomach. As he felt the giant double forward, he snapped back his own head.

And he experienced a deep sense of satisfaction. He did not like paid musclemen. He had felt his shoe hit the toe, his elbow dig deep into the hard stomach, and his skull smash against the softer features of Anton's face. He had scored on all three. Not even this big monkey could take all that and still come out fighting.

In those long seconds, Martin too saw his chance. The men with the guns were all temporarily distracted.

Mr. Rogo was escaping. Jason, he saw out of the corner of his eye, had gone for Hely and was dragging her by the arm across the floor.

"Quick!" he screamed to his little group. "This way!" He grabbed Coby and swung her around to the companionway and pushed her.

Her feet missed the rungs of the ladder at the side and she crashed down. Klaas lowered himself quickly through and jumped. "Come on, Manny!" Martin shouted. The older man was kneeling. Incredibly, he seemed to be trying to pick something up. Martin shouted to him again and then jumped through the hole.

It was the instinct to flee. It hit them all and there was no resistance: Bela, the gunmen, the tiger, Martin, all of them propelled by the one overwhelming thought —escape.

Martin was the first on his feet, helping up the Dutch girl. She was crying, and her young woman's face looked childish again. Klaas too grunted and heaved himself up with the lantern he still held in his hand. They were in a dark, narrow corridor. One body in their tangled pile did not move. They looked down. It was the *Komarevo* man. His shoulder was a pulp of blood and cloth. Half his face had been torn off. His teeth grinned madly where the flap of his cheek was ripped open. Coby wailed when she saw it, and Klaas put his arm around her again.

She peered in terror up the corridor. "Where's that horrible animal?" she asked.

Martin, more familiar with the surroundings, squinted into the darkness. Beyond the corridor he could see through an open doorway into the boiler room, and beneath his feet the conduits and pipes that lined what had once been the ceiling. "Listen," he said, tilting his head to concentrate. "I can hear it. It's running away. Come on, it's clear for us to get out of here. It'll be miles ahead now." He took Coby's hand and the three of them set off, back down into the deep belly of the sinking ship.

In the seconds they had used for their escape, Rogo had freed himself and Jason had grabbed the girl. As soon as Rogo heard the dull grunt of pain behind him and felt the iron fingers relax, he too made for the companionway. He could hear Jason behind him and saw Manny Rosen on his hands and knees. At least, he thought, the odds will be better for us in that labyrinth of corridors and rooms.

"Stop!" It was Bela. He had stabilized himself by grabbing a bracket on the side of the hull with his left hand. The ladder was knotted around his legs and his off-balance body stood out from the ship at a sharp angle. But he was no longer rocking, and his right arm, thrust through the rungs, held the heavy Stechkin perfectly steady. He aimed at Rogo.

"A tiger!" He laughed. His face was white and taut and there was hysterical relief in the laugh. "You must have known, all of you. Brilliant, quite brilliant! But not successful, I fear. It doesn't matter now. I shall kill you as I should have killed you from the start."

Jason slid in front of the girl. Rogo's eyes checked the distance to the companionway and the distance to Bela. Should he try to jump down the hole, or should he chance rushing Bela? Either way he would get shot.

The respectful, courteous tones of the retired hardware dealer sounded ludicrous. "No you won't, Mr. Bela, because I'll shoot you if you try."

They all turned. Manny was still on his knees hold-

ing Rogo's pistol in both hands, the barrel pointing
without a quiver at Bela's chest. He appeared to be
praying with a small Colt in his hands.

"Go ahead, Mr. Rogo," he said, as deferential as
ever. "You get out with the rest and I'll keep an eye
on him."

The thoughts clicked through Rogo's mind like people through a busy turnstile. It was his gun. It was not
working. Manny knew it was not working. But Bela
didn't. Rogo's grin was triumphant. But the minute any
action started they would be lost. They had only seconds. Bela had merely to turn his pistol a few inches to
take a shot at Manny. The gunman in the corner
stopped sobbing; he was coming back to reality.

"You're a killer, Manny, a real killer." He dropped
down the hole, swinging through on his hands.

"Quick!" Jason pulled Hely over the rubble. She
slipped swiftly down the steps and Jason called out
"Come on, Manny, now," as he followed her.

Bela and Manny, the international thug and the old
shopkeeper were motionless and wordless. Bela's three
henchmen watched and waited.

Manny made no attempt to follow them. He clasped
the gun in front of him, careful to make sure it was
trained on the man on the ladder. It would give them
more time. Soon, he thought, that man is going to
turn and shoot me. As soon as he finds his nerve
he will do it. Or perhaps that man in the corner, the
one who was making the noise, will try. They were
waiting and watching and he could hear their sup-
pressed breathing. They were frightened. Frightened!
Crooks like them frightened of old Manny Rosen? He
nearly laughed. He had done it. He knew he could.

He had saved them all. Mr. Rogo would get them away somehow now.

Funny how easy it is, he thought. He had simply picked up the pistol and everything had changed. A little thing like that. Belle had never liked guns at all, but she would have approved of this. He was sure about that. Odd how everyone treats you differently when you hold a gun. These men never gave me a thought before, and now they can think of nothing else. Even if it didn't work properly. Manny was glad it would not fire. This was like pretending, like little boys with their toys. It gave everyone time to escape, but he knew he would not have to shoot. He was glad. He did not want to shoot people, even these people. What would Belle have said? He smiled. The man on the ladder was staring at him. What would she have said if she'd seen her Manny behaving like one of those television detectives? Well, soon that man Bela would take his chance and it would all be over.

He had known that from the start. He had seen it all with wonderful clarity when he had first spotted the gun. He knew he would die, and it was the right, the proper thing to do. Manny Rosen wanted to die. He wondered about Belle's medallion that she had asked him to deliver to their grandson in Israel. He would have done that, he thought, if he had wished to go on living. But he felt no desire to be on land again, to be among people, to be with his friends and family. Not without Belle. His life had ended with hers. What's a little thing like a medallion next to that? *No, it's all over now, Belle*, he said to himself, *and I'm going to join you soon*. And wouldn't she smile when she knew how he'd fooled some of the gangsters with a broken gun? He laughed himself at the thought. It was a cracked, burbling laugh, and it came more strongly when he saw the look of amazement on Bela's face. *If he only knew*, thought Manny Rosen. *If he only knew.*

The firing came almost simultaneously. Two rapid shots from Bela, swinging around quickly like a monkey on a rope. A solid, thick burst from the moustached man in the corner. Manny felt himself folding gently forward and wondered why his laugh had turned to an odd coughing sound. He did not even attempt to pull the trigger. Manny Rosen firing guns at people? Never. Never in this world.

It was Martin's first question when the two parties of three rejoined, and he knew the answer before Rogo spoke. Martin had led the Dutchman and his daughter from the passage into the boiler room. He had become so accustomed to the staggering anarchy of the upside-down liner that he was almost surprised to hear their astonishment.

Indeed, the room was a scene of spectacular chaos, fitfully illuminated by a fire which still blazed up one of the walls. The boilers had ripped free from the moorings and come crashing down. Some lay whole, like giant pods on what was now the floor. Others had broken and looked like enormous shattered eggs, on a bed of wrecked machines, dials, gauges, pipes, and pumps. Oil filmed every surface, and many times they slipped as they clambered to the far end of the room. Sometimes, too, Martin heard Coby gasp as she saw yet another still, crumpled body. Martin scarcely noticed them anymore. He was used to living in a mortuary. They got to the far end of the room, only beginning to recover from their terror, to find a doorway that led through to a corridor. Of course, Martin reminded himself, this was known to the crew as Broadway. It served all the storerooms, refrigeration departments, bakeries, stockrooms, and the hundred and one other operations that kept passengers contented. Several staircases and corridors led off it. It would be easy to hide there. So Martin, Klaas, and Coby squatted down among the rubble, prepared to start running again if those cold-faced killers came through the door.

There had been no sign of the tiger, other than the mutilated body of the gunman it had discarded. Martin had looked down Broadway. The light was poor, but he could clearly see there was no tiger there. It must have fled much farther into the ship. Perhaps it had drowned. Martin could not see where the corridor dropped into the water but he knew from the angle of the ship there could not be much more that was above the waterline. It was then that he remembered again with a brutal jolt that the ship would sink very soon. That knowledge had been swept away by the menace of the guns and the shock of the wild animal. How were they going to get out? They were trapped.

He saw Rogo's head come tentatively through the doorway across the room.

He saw the young American and the girl in the wet suit. Her flashlight lit the way ahead. There was no Manny. He asked, and Rogo explained in short bursts as he struggled towards them.

"They got him. We heard the shots." Rogo paused

for a moment and wiped his brow with an oily hand. He held his palm out. "What'd he do a crazy thing like that for? He knew the stinking gun was bust."

He was upset. He had liked Manny. He had liked both the Rosens. If Rogo had ever needed to justify his work as a policeman, he would have seen himself as defending people like the Rosens. The little people, the poor people, the honest people, they all needed someone like Rogo to see they did not get pushed around. It seemed wrong that a quiet old guy like that should die for him. He began climbing again, edging around a boiler, then stepping carefully over the jumbled mess.

"Why'd he do it, Martin? For Chrissakes, it was suicide."

"That's exactly what it was, Mr. Rogo," Martin said, reaching out a hand to pull the policeman up a step to the platform where they waited. "He didn't want to live without his Belle. You know how those two were."

He turned to Coby, "They really loved each other, miss. Manny and Belle." Then he explained to Klaas. "I knew it, I could see it in his eyes. He wanted to die, and he saved us all in doing so."

Rogo scratched his head. "You never know, d'ya? Guy like that, helluva nice guy, but who'd take him for a hero? You shoulda seen it, Martin, the way he stood all those punks off."

The moment of reflection was broken by the distant sound of voices. Hastily the group covered the last few scrambling steps out of the boiler room and into the the wide long corridor called Broadway. It certainly came as no surprise to Rogo and company, but the others, who had not experienced the hostile strangeness of this upside-down world before were shocked and astounded at the unreality of it all. The mass of tubes and pipes and conduits that almost covered the ceiling were now underfoot and made any kind of progress slow and tricky. What little light there was had to penetrate to the central corridor through the maze of rooms and cubicles and stores. The smell was appalling. To the dank stench left by the sea were added the smells from the contents of stockrooms, food and drink and supplies of all kinds that had been pitched into that unholy brew when the ship capsized. Hely's light flicked quickly away from the bundled bodies which lay sometimes singly, sometimes in tragic, lifeless mounds of two or three.

They had gone about twenty yards when Rogo stopped the procession. Now was the time for thinking, and they must be quick. It was to Jason primarily that he put his plan and he was plainly looking for his approval.

"How about this, cowboy?" he said. "Martin knows this crazy tub a bit—he takes Klaas and the girls further down into the ship and finds somewhere to hide while we fix a welcome for those bastards."

Jason agreed, "Yep, that's about all we can do. One thing, though. Hely stays with me. We've got quite a double act going here and we don't want to break it up now. Anyway, I might need someone to let a tiger loose again." His arm slid around her hips.

"Okay," Rogo was saying, and squinting nervously ahead. "I'd like to know where that goddamn tiger went to. It ain't my idea of fun."

His anxiety was reflected in Klaas's comment. "Mr.

Rogo, I fear we have made a terrible mistake in running down here. The ship is sinking. That animal is loose. We are trapped."

The suggestion of incompetence pricked Rogo's temper. "You got any better idea? If we'd stayed back there, we'd been shot for sure. At least we got a chance here."

"What chance?" This time it was Martin.

"Okay, I'll tell you," said Rogo. "Those guys are going to come looking for us. Me and Jason can maybe jump them. With a couple of their guns we can shoot our way past those little sailor boys. See?"

"He's right." Rogo was relieved to hear Jason's backing. "It's not so hot, I know, but it's the only hope we've got. Rogo and I can pick our spot here, the rest of you find the best cover you can until it's over."

His words seemed to give everyone some small hope. Coby offered, "I'd like to stay with you, Jason. I'm not afraid." She saw his grin and resented it. It was the smile of encouragement you give to a child.

"Thanks, Coby, but you'd better go with Martin there," he said. She was about to protest when they heard shouting in the distance. It sounded like Bela. Rogo turned Jason to him and hoarsely whispered, "Okay, Jason, you can keep the broad with you, that's your business. But it's you and me in this setup. We're the only ones who can take these guys. I got to trust you, but I'm not sure I like it."

"Who got you out of the last tight corner, Batman?"

"Yeah, well thanks for that, but I still got a lotta questions for you, Jason. Right now they'll wait."

The easy teasing was back in Jason's voice. "All it takes is a little faith, Batman."

"And stop calling me Batman, for Chrissakes."

It was not the old fierce anger this time. The fire of their initial antagonism had died, although the distrust remained. There was no common ground between them in philosophy or temperament, but they had each seen in the other one quality to respect: courage. Their exchanges were acquiring the rhythm of an uncertain courtship.

There was something almost like friendship in Jason's reply: "Don't worry, Rogo. We'll swing a couple of surprises on those monkeys."

He was looking into the rooms which went off the corridor, peering into the darkness and examining them. "Let's have some light in here, Hely. Ah, this is mine."

It was the hairdressing salon. As they both looked in, Jason whispered to her, "Can I interest madame in a coiffure?"

Rogo too was stumbling from door to door. "Goddamn kook!" he said, thinking aloud. "Batman, for God's sake!" He raised his voice and called back to Jason, "I guess you realize that makes you Robin!"

The tiny cinema was exactly what Rogo had been looking for. It was nearly pitch black. There were only about a dozen rows of seats and they were still anchored firmly to what was now the ceiling, their hinged backs hanging down like flags on a windless day. It had been a low room and Rogo could almost touch the seats when he reached up. It was ideal for the plan he had half-formulated in his mind. Rogo knew all about traps. He had walked into too many in his life not to know the simple mechanics and devices that made them work. A trap was a conjuring trick:

you made the audience look at your left hand while your right hand was doing the work. Simple. He edged cautiously into the black room. His foot jammed against a soft, heavy object. He felt around with his foot. There were several bodies. There was also a chair. That should be enough. He felt almost happy. Danger did not worry him as long as he could fight back. The tiger had terrified him because of the unexpected nature of its power. Under Bela's gun he had suffered the frustration of not being able to retaliate. Now it was a straight battle, whatever the odds, and Mike Rogo had never backed off a scrap in his life. He had Jason, too. Martin was a plucky little guy, but he did not have the experience—the ringcraft, they called it when Rogo was a boxer—for this sort of setup. Klaas was not a fighting man, it was as simple as that. But everything about Jason, the set and style of the man, suggested someone who could handle himself. The way he had stood in the tiger's path. That took nerve, real nerve. Rogo decided he had been right. Jason was a fighting man okay. For the moment that freaky guy seemed to be on his side and Rogo was grateful. The questions would have to wait. Batman! Who the hell did he think he was?

Rogo unclipped the suspenders that held up his evening dress trousers. The trousers sagged onto his hips. He had wanted to wear a belt but Linda had insisted on suspenders. It was the last favor the poor kid had done him and even then she had said she would not go to dinner with him looking like the garbage man. Funny, he thought, now it might save his life. You never know, you just never know. His trousers began to slide down and he grabbed them and cursed with clinical fluency in the darkness.

* * *

The bizarre effects of the inversion of the *Poseidon* were nowhere more ludicrously dramatic than in the hairdressing salon. Hely's light revealed an extraordinary world of familiar objects made suddenly strange. The large, thickly padded chairs hanging from their elegant chromium-plated stalks. From the hand-basins, also still in position, the plugs dangling foolishly on their chains. The floor was buried in piles of wigs, hairnets, curlers, bottles, lotions, shampoos, combs, and brushes.

Jason was examining the room for possibilities. "Yeah, this will do," he said. "The problem is, I can fix a trap okay, but how do we get the rat to walk in?"

"How do you mean?" Hely was checking the details of their surroundings.

"Well," he explained, "he's going to come through that door pretty warily even if we aren't armed. And if he sees me before I zap him . . ." He turned his index finger into a gun barrel.

Hely said, "I can make him walk into your trap."

He looked puzzled. "How?"

"The oldest way in the world." Hely drew down the zip on the front of her wet suit. It fell apart. Her bared body glowed in the gray shadows. "It might take his mind off things for a minute."

Jason slipped his hands inside the opened jacket and felt the taut bow of her back curve in his hands. She was like a coiled spring, and her body kicked in his hands as she moved against him. She angled her moving mouth against his. Then she leaned back to focus on his face.

"Right from the start I knew I wanted you," she said. "I saw something in you. Rogo saw it, that's why he is nervous of you. You and that tiger, that was the bravest thing I have ever seen in my life. Want me, Jason, please want me too."

"You sure as hell pick some funny places to turn a guy on." There was none of the usual flippancy in his tone. "Yes, I do want you, Hely. We're the same kind of people. We're special people. You and me, we're going to be alone together."

It was the rare compact between two solitary people who had never known the passive emotion of need. They simply saw and took, with the mutual recognition of champions meeting. His hands on her back, their words sealed an understanding made in the shadow of death.

But Hely could not forget the purse on her belt. In it were the rings and other jewelry that might betray her. She had to find out if Jason was ruthless as well as strong. His tough handling of the policeman indicated he was no great respecter of law and order. But the sharpness of his detestation for Bela appeared to reflect some deeply held principles. Hely had to know.

"You could have made a deal with Bela," she said. "Why didn't you? Is it because he kills for money?"

His arms held her loosely. His face crinkled into a grin. "No, not really. I don't care too much about what the world calls moral anymore. I used to, believe me. But world morality once called me a hero, then made me a killer and despised me for it. Morality's like the weather. Don't ever count on it."

Her hands lightly stroked his face. "I don't understand," she said still searching.

His eyes went over her head and there was an old

remembered hurt in them. "Vietnam? Okay? They sent me out there. To fight for freedom, to kill the baddies in the black hats and run the outlaws out of town. I did. Then they decided the guys in black hats weren't such baddies after all, gave them the town, and my status sort of shifted from hero to murderer in one go."

Hely began to see. She asked, "Does it matter what people think?"

His voice had a dreary distant note. "No, I don't suppose so. But it matters what I think of me. I shot up a helluva lot of those little brown guys out there because I thought *they* were the killers. Now everyone says they were nice, home-loving, tax-paying citizens who just wanted to run their own country their own way. So what do I do? Give the kiss of life to all the ones I killed? And me, I'm one of those kinda friendly fellas, you know. I got to know one of them real well. Used to go for a beer with him. Taught him how to play poker. Met his family. He was a great little guy. When he used to worry about what would happen, I'd say 'Don't worry, Uncle Sam's right behind you on this one. We'll see you through.' The day we quit I went out on a chopper. I could see him in the crowd, that little brown face round like a coin. He was watching. He didn't wave or beg to come or call me a traitor, but I knew all those things just the same. We left him. Correction: *I* left him. The Cong were bound to get him. I see that face a lot when I close my eyes."

She was talking to an honest man. The cold realization struck through the heat of her emotion for him. Hely knew he must never find out about the contents of the purse. He could never accept it. Whatever he was doing now, however illegal, it could surely never encompass her sort of life. But it would be all right. He would never know.

"What about me?" It was Hely's last question. "You don't know anything about me. I could be another Bela. I could be a robber or a killer or a whore."

Amusement lit up his eyes. "You know what they say, even if you've never seen gold before you'll know it when you clap eyes on it. You're gold."

She kissed him again, this time quite demurely, and knew she was safe.

The voices down the corridor of Broadway carried to them. "Quick!" Jason snapped. "You know what to do. You hook 'em, I'll bop 'em."

The proprietor of the haberdashery store in Anaheim was exceedingly upset. Martin stood in the doorway of the ship's library and tried to assess the wreckage in the poor light, and considered how unfairly the world treated him. The wreckage was complete. When the ship turned turtle, and in the subsequent movements, the shelves which would once have lined the room tidily had been flung all over what was once the ceiling. Books were scattered everywhere. They were piled in soaking mounds. There were chairs and tables, some splintered and broken. One bookcase, inexplicably, had survived almost intact. A few stubborn screws still held it against a wall, retaining virtually all its load of books. It looked incongruously neat in that scene of anarchy.

"We should be okay here," said Martin, leading in Coby and her father.

It was, he thought, an insult. Whenever there was danger of any kind, he was always placed among the noncombatants, with the old men and the women. He was as brave as any of them. Rogo had been more afraid of the tiger than he had. He would have stood up to Bela just as gallantly as the others, given the chance. But they always put him at the back. It was the humiliating course of his life yet again. Poor little James! Don't play with the rough boys, James. You're too little for the football team, James. Don't argue, he's bigger than you, James. All his life he had had sand kicked in his face, and now they were doing it again. They had packed him off with the peaceful Dutchman and the young girl and told him to hide until it was all over. He was angry and, as usual, no one had even noticed.

He had shepherded Klaas and the girl along Broadway until they met the water. They had almost walked into it. This was where the sea took over and lay still, quiet, evil, waiting to claim the rest of the ship. Then he had led them back to the first room that was clear of the water. They must be, he judged, about seventy yards further down into the ship than Rogo and Jason. Well, he had done as he had been told. He had found them a refuge.

The girl's fingers were locked around his arm. She was very pretty, he thought. He felt her fingers almost encircle his arm, and again the pain of the insult came back to him. She could hardly have spanned Rogo's arm with both her hands. And he had seen the way her eyes hung on Jason. No one had ever looked at James Martin like that. He patted her fingers and said, "Don't worry, I'll look after you." It sounded quite manly.

Her fingers squeezed him. "Thank you," she said. "I know that Jason is going to get us all out of this mess. Don't you think he is an extraordinary man?"

A lifetime's secret resentment burned in him against all the Jasons he had known. "I wouldn't be too sure about him, miss. We don't even know why he came here. I certainly wouldn't want to rely on a person like him. He looks like a crook to me."

"Oh no!" Coby was aghast. "No, no. He saved us back there, didn't he?"

Martin knew he would regret it even as he delivered the words. But not even his sense of shame could prevent it. "I think he was more interested in saving that blonde, and I guess we all know why."

Little girl protest matured swiftly into grown woman's spite. "If you mean," said Coby, "that she's been chasing him since the minute she set eyes on him, then . . ."

The first scream chopped her off in midstream. It was high and shrill, sustained on one note until it faded for lack of breath. It was followed by a second, then a third. It was a scream of complete madness. There was no mind directing the noise. It was coming from inside the library.

THE TRAPS

9

Captain Bela looked with great distaste at the gray
crescent of oil which marked his cuff. It was messy.
The whole operation had become messy. Captain Bela,
who always liked to boast that his work was like his
cuffs, clean and impeccable, was irritated that neither
appeared to be so at that moment.

He was standing in the hold. The beam from his
torch showed quite clearly the prize which had drawn
him to the *Poseidon*, but the moment of triumph was
marred. The packing cases, strongly nailed and wired
together, had almost all survived the buffetings of the
ship. One, thrown on its end in the corner behind
the door, had smashed open, and through the splinters

of wood had fallen several ingots of gold. Bela picked
one up in his left hand. It took the light from the
flash and turned into a soft mellow flame. It was so
small and slim, like a bar of chocolate. Stamped in
the metal were the words "one kilo gold" and yet
it must be worth four thousand dollars. And there also
printed into the metal the famous "four nines"—999.9.
Even gold itself was not complete perfection, Bela
thought. But he knew it had a magic that lay beyond
its dimension and value. Gold, he thought, was like
a woman. You could set down on paper all her attri-
butes, but you could not measure the power of her
beauty. Gold and women: the incalculables, the im-
measurables, the currency of power.

He kept the bar in his hand as he headed back
towards the square of blue sky where his men had
cut through into the ship. The gold was there for
the taking, without a doubt. Most of it would be
returned to his employers in Athens, and he would
be handsomely rewarded for his efficiency and silence.
But since no one would dare risk arguing about it,
Captain Bela felt that several of the bars would be
lost, and his Swiss bank account show a surprising
improvement.

He used the knuckles of his flashlight hand to
balance as he stepped over the smashed chunks of
metal, softly cursing the sheer untidiness of the whole
business. It was, he thought, the tragedy of the Western
countries that they failed even to understand the crude
laws on which they constructed their own philosophies.
They could not even grasp the cornerstone of their
own childish ethic: the market price. This had been
a case in point. Jason held a reasonable bargaining
position: Bela had offered him the price that situation

required. But the American had then reacted on some irrational impulse that had thrown the whole thing into confusion. Jason was a romantic, and Bela cursed his own stupidity for trying to deal with him. Those people always introduced purely subjective emotions into what was a straightforward business transaction. They were unpredictable. And yet, Bela sighed, the Americans were supposed to be the great capitalists who understood the disciplines of trade.

He should not have been surprised. He had heard of Jason's work around the Mediterranean and he should have recognized the unprincipled actions of a woolly-minded romantic. He seemed to sail in and out of the law as much as Bela. His work certainly seemed as dangerous. But whereas he, Bela, worked to a clear set of rules that were governed by the market price, Jason did not.

Bela had first come across him when the *Komarevo* had been taking Greek Cypriots off the island at the time of the Turkish invasion. There were people who needed to move quickly and quietly, there were arms shipments. Some men who had paid for deliverance saw Bela's smile as he took a second payment, and handed them over to their enemies. That was business. Jason too had been moving people and guns, but often, by all accounts, without any reward at all. It caused confusion. It spoiled the market for professional men like Bela. It was inefficient. Jason was an American and could have no interest, either personal or political, in the squalid lives of those who could not manage their affairs properly. There were other stories, too, of the blond American taking a hand in the illicit commerce of the seas, stories of bravery and daring, and Captain Bela knew that he was a man who was respected. A capitalist who worked at a loss—no wonder the West was cracking!

Bela slid the flat ingot onto a shelf formed by a shattered catwalk beside the rope ladder. That one bar would pay his tailor's bills for a while. But for the moment he must impose some order on this business. He had made mistakes, and he must correct them urgently. He should never have been tempted to reason with Jason. He should have killed him immediately. True, Jason did have many friends, and perhaps Bela would have to slip behind the Iron Curtain and endure that spartan life for a little while. That would be an inconvenience, but Jason must die. So too must the policeman. That was clearly agreed in his contract.

His other mistake was in losing his temper. Bela never lost his temper. That was his finest quality. He held on to his composure and kept his wits clear. This time, for once, he had failed, and it irked him. Perhaps it was Jason's bantering tone, perhaps that obdurate policeman, perhaps it was the shock of the tiger or the stupidity of that old man holding a gun on him. Whatever the accumulation of motives, he had quite lost control when he saw them escaping into the rest of the ship, and had screamed at Anton and the others to catch them. He could have left them to sink with the ship, as it surely must soon, or killed them as they tried to return. There had been no need to take the risk of hunting them. Still, Anton and his crew were highly professional, and Jason's ragbag friends were not armed; they should be able to clear the matter up easily.

Very well, he thought. There were now only two considerations. First, the gold must be moved. He must have ten or twelve men from the *Komarevo* to transport the bars back to his vessel as quickly as possible. And they must be properly armed to deal with Jason and the rest if any of them escaped Anton. Too much time had been lost already.

A light smile appeared on his slim, intelligent features. Despite the difficulties, he had clarified the problem quite simply. He scaled the rope ladder with deft, quick steps, and was giving out orders to the man in the pinnace even as he swung a leg over the top. It was all falling neatly into place again. The smile vanished. A button had been torn off his blazer.

Half running, half climbing, bumping and clawing their way, Anton and the two other gunmen sped as best they could over the unhelpful wreckage of the boiler room. They had been whipped into action by Bela's shouts of rage—"After them, you oafs! Kill them! What are you, little girls?" They had never before seen the captain in such a fury and it had sent them tumbling down the companionway and on into the ship as fast as they could.

Anton was worried. It was apparent even to him that things were not going to plan, and now it was confirmed by Captain Bela's rage. He was the first to the open door at the opposite end of the boiler room and he paused, panting, to shine his light down into the corridor which lay in front. His nose was bleeding. He had an ache in his stomach. His toe hurt. The policeman had tricked him. Anton had not had any games with him. He thought with warm pleasure of the enjoyment he would have when he caught the little policeman and twisted his body. He would enjoy hearing the policeman scream.

It took him several seconds to realize that the

scream he was hearing was real, and not the one in his daydreams. It was a long, high wail, followed by two more, and it came from down at the far end of the corridor, well beyond the vague shapes of the walls and doors he could see in his light. It must be one of those two girls. They must be hiding right down there at the bottom. Anton wanted to be the first to find them, simply for the pleasure of it, and for the reward of Captain Bela's smile.

He set off, slipping and half falling on the uneven footing, down into the darkness. He would find them. Then tonight there would be fun and money and girls and vodka.

The other two watched him go. The man with one eye—the other was a closed flap—had lost his gun in the panicky scramble when the tiger came out. He had retrieved it and now its menacing aim followed his flashlight down the corridor. "Let him go," he said. "We take it more careful. They're not armed, but no chances, huh?"

The second agreed. He was a thin-faced, pale man, a moustache weakly hanging on his upper lip. He too had been stunned by the frightening sequence of events in the engine room. But at least he had recovered in time to shoot the old man. He also had his flash in one hand, his automatic in the other. "Anton, he's crazy," he mumbled.

Shoulders nervously hunched, they worked their way warily into Broadway. They ignored the bodies their feet bumped against; dead men held no terrors for them. They ignored too the windless stench of the place.

The man with one eye took the left-hand side. There were several doors, mostly open, in the first few yards.

He stood boldly in the doorway of the first; there was little to fear. It had been a storeroom which was now a jumble of broken shelves and scattered tins. There was nowhere anyone could hide. He checked two more, each one revealing nothing. His companion was several yards ahead, with fewer rooms to search, and was now only a scuffling shadow.

The next room took longer. It was the children's playroom. That meant they must be moving from the part of the corridor which housed the unseen services to the public facilities. He kicked over a toy house which had landed on its side. Then he searched behind a huge shiny slide. Nothing.

The next door was already open. Again he stood boldly. The extraordinary topsy-turvy scene had only begun to reassemble itself in his mind as a hairdressing salon when his light picked out the girl. He flicked his gun up quickly. She was standing against the far wall, her arms flung open and her hands empty. Her wet suit was unzipped, and the browns and golds of her body burned like flames in the cold black coffin of the ship. Her stance, feet apart, head thrown back, unsmiling mouth parted, was unequivocal. She held out one hand and with all four fingers beckoned him. Her body arched backwards, a switch of silver hair flickered across her shoulder. He began to walk, mesmerized, towards her, the light, the gun, his one eye, all on that tense and bending body.

There is a fraction of time so small that the mind can only record a picture, without analyzing or rationalizing it. He saw clearly the girl. He saw too that into his picture there came a leg. From above, out of the blackness. What seemed a single, amputated leg. And it was moving fast. For all that, his eye recorded the faded blue of the denim, whitening at the knee. That was all. The two fantasies, of half-naked girl and dismembered limb, blew apart as the foot stabbed into his throat. It hit deep and hard, just below the chin. He gave a small cough as people do to attract attention, and slumped over backwards. His fantasies died with him.

Jason knew the short, slashing blow had connected properly as his foot sank into the softness of the neck and felt the snap as the man's head kicked back. He let go of the chair suspended from the ceiling, where he had been clinging like a monkey, and dropped to the floor lightly.

He turned the man over. One eye stared at him. Jason closed it with a delicate finger. He was dead. "Well," he said, "I guess he won't be chasing the chicks anymore. You were great, Hely. You sure staged one hell of an act there. I nearly forgot to jump the bastard."

Hely said, "That wasn't an act, Jason." He looked over his shoulder. She went on, "No, Jason. It was for you. Now!"

The tone was imperative. Jason rose and advanced towards her. They both saw in that blinkered moment the force that drove them together. It was beyond attraction and love. It was beyond even strength and sexuality. It was one of those few dark, undeniable, elemental powers that cross all moralities and codes —that raw instinct that canceled all others. It was life and death, together. And for a time the whole earth revolved around the axis of their spinning, greedy bodies, until at last they sank into each other's exhausted arms.

As natural as the cries and gasps that had come

from her throat, the tears then came from Hely's eyes. She sobbed joyously on his shoulder. She cried, and cried again in delight at her own tears. She had discovered something in herself—the capacity to feel. She was no longer independent. She was no longer free. She was no longer untouched by the world around her. She was part of it, and she wept.

She would throw the rings away, she thought. They no longer mattered. She lay in the crook of his lap as he sat, knees up, back against the wall, her tears warm on her cheek. His voice spilled over her, comforting and warm.

He was talking about his early life. It was all about a small town somewhere, a sunny place where fish took boys' hooks, and it seemed right that they should. He talked too of men called slants and gooks who suddenly seemed to have thoughts and feelings and families like him, and a friend who went fishing with him, and the fish took the hooks just the way they did back in his small town, and the friend, the man who never waved or spoke as the helicopter left, but stayed to die.

He spoke of what he called "the little people," the victims of vast international policies, whose lives were upturned at the stroke of a dictator's pen or the whim of a fickle electorate half a world away. The little people all around the world whose lives are exposed in the name of expediency.

His voice came through her trance. "All they taught me was warfare. I can fire any gun in the field, I can drive a tank, I can fly a chopper, I can sail a boat, I can climb a mountain, and I can kill with my bare hands. That's my craft. Only now I try to use it to straighten out a debt I can't repay in full."

Some of it she understood. But all of it revealed a man who was propelled by belief. That belief would change her life as surely as it had changed his.

The moustache had not grown as he had hoped. With the back of his flashlight hand, he brushed it and it felt soft and feminine. It was not easy to be a respected killer at the age of twenty if you could not even produce a virile moustache.

He kicked open the door on his right. It looked like a small theater. From the corridor, his flash beam revealed little of the inside, and he waited for a moment. He was anxious to accomplish this job well and was prepared to be cautious.

So far it had not been a good day. He was tired of the other members of the crew of the *Komarevo* teasing him about his age, his slight build, and the not absolutely essential morning shave. What was it Bela had said? "It looks like a baby mouse that lay down and died." The others had laughed.

Then there had been the tiger. He had not run away, it was true, but he had frozen in the corner, the Stechkin useless in his hand. He had recovered only in time to shoot that stupid old man with the pistol, and the captain had also got in two shots at him. Captain Bela had been furious about the way things were going wrong. This was his chance to recover the situation for his boss. There were only four men and two girls, all unarmed, and he would run them down and destroy them. Then Bela would respect him, and the others would stop treating him like a child.

He walked slowly through the doorway. His right hand was ready on the trigger. His left, holding the light, also supported the gun. There would be no mistakes.

Yes, it was a theater. His light, clumsily angled upwards, revealed the dangling seats. It was odd, this upside-down feeling everywhere. The dead air was unmoving. He had to brace his legs to hold his position on the ceiling, cambered by the angle of the ship. His feet inched forward until they stopped against a heavy, inert object. He knew what it would be. A body. On the blurred rim of the beam he could see three or four of them. men, judging by their clothes. Two of them appeared to be in dinner jackets. Another was in an undershirt. What had he been doing at midnight on New Year's Eve that entailed being half-dressed? Well, at least he would have died happy.

Something was wrong about the seats above his head. One of them, only one, was not hanging down. There was a tape or something hanging from it. The seat suddenly crashed down, and he felt his nerves prick and his stomach hollow and dropped into a crouch. The gun and light pointed at the seat. Why had there been that sudden movement? His left leg rested on the back of one of the bodies, the one in the undershirt. Eyes, light, gun, nerves, everything was directed to that seat which completed the perfect symmetry of the row, like inverted gravestones.

The movement of the seat had been odd. There was something else odd too. Even as he realized what it was, it was too late. It was the body beneath his leg: it was *warm*. But before he had a chance to work on the thought he found himself being catapulted into the air and across the room. The body beneath him had thrown him three or four yards away. He landed on his face, his arms and legs flying, and for a moment felt himself spinning on a surface of glass, like a fallen skater. His Stechkin had gone. Where was his gun? Still spinning, he wildly swung the light around. He moved it too quickly and the beam skimmed over the unhelpful shadows. The gun must be nearby somewhere. Frantically he saw the dead man rising. The bulky figure in the underwear shirt was heading toward him, a menacing, waddling figure, with arms bent, holding a rope or something. He grasped the light in both hands, half sitting up, to steady it. He must find the Stechkin before that living corpse got to him.

The now steady beam found it, cool and black and polished. It had come to rest about four yards to his left, against the wall. Two leaps, two frog leaps from this position, and he would reach it. But there was no time. The advancing figure was almost upon him. Then there was a crashing, splintering sound. The pounding figure sank a foot into the ground. He saw the look of stupefaction on his pursuer's face and saw him lift enraged, imploring hands and cry, "Sweet Suffering Jesus!" Of course, the lights! The theater lights were concealed in glass-fronted boxes built flush into the ceiling. That was the glass surface he had traversed. The bulky man had crashed through. He was imprisoned around his calves by jagged knives of glass.

Bela's man spluttered a mad laugh of triumph and leaped towards the gun. He landed halfway there and immediately sprang again. But the trapped man grabbed his own legs and tore them free of the savage glass teeth and sprang towards him.

Desperately Bela's man scrabbled to regain his gun. It was still warm from his previous grip. But his panting pleasure exploded into a scream of pain as he felt two battering-ram knees punch into the small of his back. He felt a dry, stubbly material across his face, and then stretch and tighten round his neck. There was no air now, not even the poisonous air there had been before; white lights came behind his eyes and his tongue turned to a balloon. Then the blinding lights in his head went out.

Rogo stayed on his back for a whole minute afterwards, holding his suspenders stretched as tightly as he could. Then he slid off and spun the dead man over. He saw a small weasel face with what might have been a moustache or just a careless shave. He was only a kid. Festooned around his neck were Rogo's suspenders, and the light showed the decorative horses that pranced down them.

Linda had bought them for his Christmas present. When was that? A week ago. She got them with horses because she said they had class. Horses! Class! Horseback riding ain't my style, Rogo remembered saying, but it was no use. Linda was dead now, and Rogo had killed a man with the suspenders. Well, one thing you gotta give good-class suspenders: they don't bust when you strangle guys with them. He unwound his gift and stood up.

The trap had worked. Just a pair of suspenders and a movie seat. It was the oldest trick in the world. Get the guy to look the other way and then hit him. He'd fallen for it all the way. Christ, he thought, but that had been close when the kid just about sat on him. Rogo had been worried for a second then. And those goddamn panel lights! He felt the warmth creeping into his shoes. He took the light from the man's unprotesting fingers and shone it down. His evening dress pants, filthy, greasy and shapeless, were now shredded below the knees. He looked like a castaway. Blood rose through the long, straight lacerations that fringed his legs. The hell with it, he thought. Mike Rogo ain't no ballerina anyway.

THE TUNNEL OF DEATH

10

It was the sight of that familiar freckled face that snapped the screaming woman out of her hysterics.

"You remember me," Martin pressed, holding her face in his hands. "Mr. Martin. You know, the Mr. Martin who kept on pestering for vitamin pills?"

"Oh, Mr. Martin!" She groaned with relief. "Oh, Mr. Martin, you and those pills. And I told you they didn't do a scrap of good."

He grinned up at Coby and Klaas as they gathered round the sobbing woman in the library. "I haven't had any since dinner last night and I'm doing okay. You must've been right."

As soon as the shock of the screams had worn off,

they had seen where they were coming from. They had picked their way through the mounds of books to the furthermost corner of the library where the slumped body shuddered and groaned.

At first Martin did not recognize her. She was soaking and filthy. The impeccable white uniform he remembered was now a torn, stained rag. The jauntily authoritative hat gone. The hair, formerly severe, straggled around her face, greased with water and oil. It was hard to imagine that this defeated, whimpering creature had been the affable despot he had known as the ship's nurse. He had last seen her with the doctor leading a group of passengers along Broadway towards the bow of the ship. They had insisted that it was the only way to escape. What had happened to them all?

Talk of Martin and his pills jerked her back to reality. She sat up and looked at the little group. At the sight of Coby, another woman, however young, she made a futile attempt to shape the drenched wreckage of her hair. Then she explained. She had been sent by the doctor to bring up the rear of their column of refugees, and they had headed towards the rescue they were confident awaited them. The water hit them quite unexpectedly when the doctor opened a watertight door, and the force of the inrushing flood had swamped them.

She had managed to run a little way before the waters caught her and swept her back along Broadway. The currents that must have swirled through the ship had taken her into the library, and she lay clinging on the top of the shelves in a bubble of air that remained when the water level settled. With the ship's last shift of angle, the sea had been sucked from the room, and she simply dropped to the ceiling. She had lain there since, terrified, disorientated, sobbing, and screaming.

She was fast recovering the self-possession of her training, and Martin was beginning to explain the new circumstances, when they heard the heavy clumping of feet and bumping and cursing in the corridor. The oaths were not in English. One of Bela's men must have penetrated the traps.

They listened anxiously.

"There's nothing we can do by ourselves, is there?" Coby said.

Martin's irritation was fueled even further when Klaas said to him, "How can we fight them if they have guns?"

"Well," Martin was pleased to hear that his thin voice sounded quite firm. "We're on our own now. We must try to fight. Don't be afraid, Coby, they've only got two arms and legs like us, you know."

He checked their faces for the confidence he was seeking to inspire. There was none. He understood. It was hard for them to feel confidence in a little guy with red hair and baby-blue eyes.

He tiptoed back nearer the door and signaled the others to follow him. The nurse got to her feet. Klaas shook his head in doubt. Coby looked at the unlikely hero with the Adam's apple bobbing in his stalk of a neck, but she followed him, and squeezed his arm in encouragement.

Even Martin's eagerness for action wavered when he saw the shape in the doorway. It was the one they had called Anton, the giant who was going to torture Mr. Rogo. Martin felt his breathing quicken.

Anton stepped in and shone his light around. This was the room, he was sure of it. And there they were.

The old seaman. The pretty girl. A woman he had never seen before. The skinny little man. He gave a chuckle, a genuinely gratified chuckle. He reached for the gun in his belt and rocked towards them.

Martin knew that was the moment. "Right, let him have it, folks!" he shouted. For one paralyzed second, he realized he had no idea what to do next. Then he snatched up a book and flung it with a twist of his wiry frame. It hit Anton just below the eye.

Anton swayed clumsily. He shifted his foot to regain balance and it slipped on a pile of soaking books. His great arms waved wildly, the flashlight beam flying around the room like a demented lighthouse.

Another volume caught him on the temple. "Great stuff, Coby!" said Martin. She had been the first to follow his example. Then Klaas too joined in, and the nurse.

Suddenly the air was thick with books. Some half open and spinning and fluttering, others cemented with water and flying as straight as rocks, and the darkened room seemed filled with them, clattering and whirling. Anton reeled around, confused by the din and blinded by the hurricane all around him. His head flinched back and his arms tried to fend off the blows as he lurched around.

Martin was whooping jubilantly. "More, more, Coby. We've got him going now!"

The nurse was recovered. She hurled a book that smacked Anton loudly on the ear. "There, you big brute!" she shouted, and pushed back a strand of dyed blonde hair.

It was a bear-baiting. Anton was the huge, powerful beast unable to come to grips with the little terriers that tormented him, and the angrier he got the less he could think clearly. His gun was gone. As he tried to hold out the light before him to see his torturers, a heavy book from Klaas's hand caught him full in the face. His balance went completely. He crashed over backwards like a demolished building. They had felled him.

Martin was beside himself with excitement. He was grinning and laughing, the wild glee of the action surging through him. They had done it. They had conquered the giant. Who needed Jason? Mr. Rogo would have to treat him with more respect after this!

Without a second thought, he snatched up a heavy volume and moved in for the kill.

There is always one terrier that goes too near the bear. Anton was not even wounded. He was dazed. He was confused. He was frustrated. He had fallen over and had now pushed himself up into a sitting position with one hand, the other still trying to ward off the raining books. But he was not injured apart from small bruises and cuts. And when he saw the keen-faced little man come hurtling at him with a book raised above his head, he swept round an arm and caught Martin's raised foot. Martin's hot-eyed excitement faded to doubt and then to terror as he landed helplessly on his back, his foot caught in a remorseless, inhuman grip.

He wriggled and squirmed and kicked but there was no release. He screamed. He could feel the bones being crushed together as though there were no flesh and sinews between them, until they seemed to be rasping on each other under the relentless pressure. He spun to his stomach, clawing at the ground to try to escape, but he heard Anton's mindless laughter and felt another huge hand clasp round his calf and drag him down. His own small white hands ran frightened through the piles of books like mice, and found no grip.

The books still bounced off Anton and blood ran from his nose into the wide gape of his grin. The laughter overflowed from him. All doubts and confusion had gone. He had hold of one of them now. He would break those little bones, then all the others, one by one. He ignored the whistling missiles around his head. They did not matter now. He ignored too the slim figure that scuttled around his side and behind him, and concentrated on pulling the twisting body into his eager arms.

Coby hurried past Anton, who was slowly drawing in his haul. She scrabbled around the mounds until she found what she knew she must have. Turning, she looked down on Anton's back, and from high above her head smashed down a beautifully bound, embossed, and massively heavy tome of the *Encyclopaedia Britannica*. It would have floored a bison.

The mad barrage stopped. Martin looked back over his shoulder. Coby looked down on the book resting between her hands.

The cry was that of a puzzled, pained child. Anton's head retreated into his turtle-neck exactly like a turtle's. He lifted his hands to contain the booming bells inside his skull, and covered his face and ears, oblivious to the rest of the world.

"Let's go," Klaas hustled the nurse towards the door. Martin, his face white as paper, crawled fearfully around Anton on all fours and Coby helped him to stand.

"Run for it, James. We must run for it now." She

was panting and pulling at his arm as Anton began to rise, still clasping his head. "Quick, or he'll get us again."

But Martin stopped in the doorway. Klaas was urging the nurse up the corridor. "Just a minute," he said. Anton was swaying towards him. The pain flickered on Martin's face as he put down his injured foot. With both hands he took hold of the back of the one set of bookshelves that was still intact. It was propped against the wall, still holding most of its contents and kept in place by a few screws. He tugged at it fiercely and felt the screws grinding in their sockets. The weight of the laden shelves began to swing out a little, then rocked back to rest against the wall. His spine felt like ice.

"He's coming, James! He'll get you again. Run, please! Please run!" He could hear Coby's anguished pleas from the doorway, and he could see Anton, tearing at the air in front of him for speed as he slipped and stumbled through heaps of books.

All the old fears welled up again inside the little shopkeeper, and again he conquered them. He did not run. He tugged once more at the side of the shelving until he felt the sharp edge bite deep into his fingers. His shoulders heaved. The whole structure of the bookshelves creaked arthritically in its joints as the last screws relinquished their hold, and the twelve-foot-high book-packed frame arced at last through the air. It shattered over Anton. Martin made for the door. His appetite for adventure was sated.

For fifteen or even twenty minutes, Rogo had waited inside the door of the theater, listening. His right hand held the gun, his left the unlit flash and his forgotten suspenders. The tiger had killed one of the thugs, he thought. He had killed another. But he was sure he had heard one go thundering down the passage earlier. Rogo was not sure how many of the *Komarevo* crew were alive, or where they were. It was not a time for risks.

He slipped gingerly out into Broadway. It was empty and silent, as far as his eyes could penetrate the half-light. He decided to check the boiler room first to see if any more of the killers were coming through, and then to see what had happened to his own party. He began to edge his way along, inch by tentative inch.

"Hands high, imperialist swine!" The hissing voice and sibilant accent were reinforced by the hard gun nuzzle in his spine. He raised his arms. At the same time he felt his trousers slipping down, and found himself in the blinding glare of a light, his gun, flash, and suspenders above his head and his legs bowed in a pair of vast, baggy underpants that touched his knees.

Jason's ringing laugh was unrestrained. "Well, you sure do believe in wrapping up against the cold, you sexy old Batman," he said. Rogo turned slowly to see the young American and the French girl, their faces wide with smiles. Jason added, "Now I would have said you were a black lace man myself. But you never can tell."

"For Chrissakes!" Rogo exploded. "You off your head or something? What the hell kind of a stunt is that to pull?" He was fastening his suspenders back on to his pants and attempting, without much success, to regain his dignity. "You get the wind coming offa the river on the night shift and those goddamn little jockey shorts ain't no good, see!"

He allowed himself a half smile. "Cut out the funny stuff. You got your fella, okay?"

"No trouble," Jason replied. "It was One-eye."

Rogo snapped on the last clip. "Well that's no big deal. Hell, there were two of you to take him."

Jason folded his arms. "Which one did you get lucky with? Not that little kid with the stick-on moustache who was crying in the corner when the tiger came out? Rogo, you ought to be ashamed. All he needed was his diaper changed."

"Yeah? Well, I didn't have to take a goddamn nanny with me!" He grinned with pride at having scored a point in the locker-room exchange.

Jason gave him the point with a wry twist of the head, and Hely's face on his shoulder smiled up at him.

"Another thing," Rogo was going on, and his glance switched between the two of them. "What the hell were you doing in there all that time?"

"We were discussing the futility of human existence and whether Muhammad Ali is open to a right cross, but I wouldn't expect a dumb cop to know anything about that," Jason countered.

"No? I guess you're right. But a dumb cop does know a coupla tricks. Like noticing a lady goes into a room with her belt on top of her rubber jacket and comes out with it underneath."

Hely looked down, frightened for a moment to be reminded of the contents of her purse. Jason glanced as well, and held his hands up. "The dumb cop isn't so dumb after all," he said.

Rogo was grinning hugely now. "You bet, cowboy. Futility of human existence!"

More seriously, Rogo held out his gun and said, "Anyway, Jason, it worked. We got this. It's not my old Police Special, but I guess it's better than that girl's gun they gave me."

"Your Police Special!" Jason sounded incredulous. "They were out-of-date at Little Big Horn, Rogo. What you've got there is a Stechkin, just about the best fully automatic pistol you can get. It's the best Russian gun anyway. Bela's boys only get the best."

Rogo was unimpressed. "A lousy Commie gun. Jesus, those Reds couldn't make catapults. Hey, where d'ya suppose that lippy guy got to, Belly or Bellhop or whatever you call the sonofabitch?"

Jason answered, "You won't see him down here, Rogo. He sends his gorillas to do the dirty work. But we're okay so far. We've got two guns and two flashlights."

"Yeah." Rogo smiled. "Now we gotta whip his ass and get that gold fast."

Hely listened quietly, wondering how the two men, so unlike and so initially hostile, now seemed to complement each other.

They were like footballers joking in the shower after the game. But it was Hely who brought them down to earth. She said, "I think we ought to try to find the others, wherever they're hiding."

Rogo's eyes narrowed. "If I got it right, that big chimp they unleashed on me is still around. Jesus, I gotta coupla points I'd like to put to him about human existence . . ."

He was interrupted by the sound of scuffling feet and sobbing. All three looked up to see the nurse picking her way along the side of the passage towards them.

"What the hell . . .?" said Rogo. "That's impossible. It's the ship's nurse."

"Quick!" she was sobbing as she ran. "The great big man. He's got that nice little Mr. Martin!"

She fell into Rogo's arms. He comforted her, and his voice was tender and understanding. "It's okay, there, don't worry. You'll be all right now, miss. Now who's got Martin and where are . . ."

Before he had time to ask, Jason was taking off down the corridor. His light deck shoes skipped nimbly over the confusion of the pipes beneath his feet. "Wait here," he called over his shoulder. "Keep an eye on him for me, Hely. You know he's scared of the dark."

With the nurse clasped around him, Rogo was helpless. He raised his eyes and shook his head. "One of these days," he sighed. "One of these goddamn days . . . Oh, for Chrissakes, he is one helluva guy, that."

"Isn't he?" said Hely. "Isn't he just one hell of a guy?"

The scene outside the library was chaotic. Everyone was talking at once and the unity that the three had had in action was shattered. Klaas was pulling at Coby and begging her to flee. She was refusing until Martin came. Little Martin, his face pinched with a mixture of terror and pain, was refusing, but not with too much conviction.

"I can get him again when he comes out," he kept saying, and wondering himself exactly what he meant by that. He shivered a little at the cursing and grunting and crashing from inside the room.

"Oh, Jason!" Coby cried, as he loped up, and Martin again experienced a twinge of resentment. He could scarcely believe it as he heard Coby jabbering excitedly, "James was so brave. He fought that great big man and beat him. You should have seen him, Captain Jason." She did not mention that she had saved him when Anton had his foot.

Jason took the situation in quickly. He looked down into the nursery-blue eyes of the smaller man and gripped his arm. "That was terrific, Martin," he said. "I knew they'd be okay with you."

Martin's modesty was itself a boast. "Well, we all got to try to do . . ."

"You fit for something else?" Jason intervened.

"You bet!" Martin snapped back.

"Can you take these two back there to Rogo?"

Martin hesitated. "I'm relying on you," Jason added.

"Okay," he said. He saw the figure appear in the doorway behind Jason and his screeched warning was almost too late.

Jason jumped to one side. The shattered shelf that Anton swung down two-handed missed his head. It would have split him wide open. Instead, it glanced off his shoulder, striking his hand. The gun went flying from his fingers and they heard it skid along the floor and then splash into invisible water. One of the guns they had fought so hard to get was lost already.

"Beat it," Jason almost whispered. Martin, with one glance at the figure outlined in the doorway, scrambled rapidly away with the other two.

Jason and Anton faced each other across the passage. The giant was leaning against the doorway, panting from his exertions. The plank in his hands was over three feet long. His woolen hat had gone and revealed hair matted with blood. One eye was swelling rapidly into an ugly lump. There was raw murder on his face. Opposite him, Jason looked an absurdly slight figure, still and quiet as he watched.

His fingertips traced the wall. A few yards down and behind him he thought he had seen a passageway that ran off at right angles. He must distract Anton and take him down there. If that maddened giant caught the others, he would tear them apart.

He must not try to fight him hand to hand. He had seen the crude strength of the man, and anyway Anton was armed with the broken shelf. He saw Anton's big eyes flickering from him to the retreating figures. Jason backed slowly. His fingers felt the wall end. The open mouth of the unknown passage was behind him. He must lure Anton to follow and somehow hope to trick him, or even just lose him.

He began to talk. Jason used the voice that people employ for dogs and children, when the tone matters more than the words. "Anton," he called softly, and the big man lifted his head at the sound of his name. "Anton, come on, boy. There's a good little boy. Come on then. Come with me."

Jason was almost purring. Anton's battered face looked baffled. He could not understand why this man was talking like that.

"Poor little Anton!" Jason kept repeating his name. "Has he bumped his head? Shall his mommy kiss it better?" He backed slowly down the corridor and Anton followed, curious and uncomprehending.

Then his tone changed. Jason straightened his back and with a contemptuous bark shouted, "You great stupid oaf, Anton! You dumbhead, Anton! You lousy lump of brainless muscle, Anton! You know what I'm saying, don't you? You've heard it all before, haven't you, Anton? Not in English maybe, but it's all the same. They call you a thickie, don't they, Anton? Don't they? Don't they?"

His voice rang around Anton's head. At first he flinched back at the ferocity of it. Then he did indeed seem to recognize the change of tone. He was fired with fury, and took three lumbering strides then swung the long plank like an ax at his tormentor.

Jason sidestepped. The wood smashed against the wall into kindling. Anton looked at the two-foot length left in his hand and began advancing towards him, the muscles of his jaw working with rage.

His feet feeling the way behind him, Jason backed down the corridor, keeping his torch on Anton to increase his confusion. He talked again, and again he taunted and jeered.

"Birdbrain, that's what they call you, isn't it, Anton? Nuts! Cracked! They all laugh at you, don't they, Anton? They think you're a big ox. And you are, a great, thick, stupid, ignorant ox."

The words seemed to strike through. Every mention of his name enraged Anton more. He stumbled forward after the light and the cruel voice. Then, throwing aside the remains of the plank, he burst into an awkward run, and his great bone-crushing hands clutched out in front of him.

Jason spun on the balls of his feet and sprinted a few yards ahead. Then he turned and sang out his sneering song.

"C'mon, crazy man. C'mon, loony! You can't catch me, can you? You're too big and dumb and clumsy!" Thrusting his own face into the light, Jason twisted his index finger against the side of his temple. It was an international mime. And it was too much for Anton. Goaded beyond bearing, he tried to rush the illuminated, mocking mask, but he was wildly off balance, and just as his hands clawed forward the light went out.

Jason had waited until the giant was almost upon him. Then he clicked the switch off, dropped on one knee and drove the heavy rubber-cased flashlight up into Anton's stomach like a truncheon. Anton doubled over and crashed to the ground.

Rolling out of the way, Jason was quickly on his feet again. For a second he thought of trying to finish the fight. But he remembered the power of the man. There was still too much strength left in that brute frame. Jason began trotting away. He would have to arm himself somehow. Failing that, he must gradually weaken him. But he must keep clear of those slaughter-house hands.

He almost stopped with surprise when he realized the change that had come over him. It was like looking in the mirror and seeing the wrong face. He grinned. Here, hunted by a murderous madman in the bowels of a sinking ship, he was experiencing an emotion he had not felt in years. He felt happy. He felt a real joy, singing in his veins. Why, he wondered, for God's sake? Why now? It could be the girl, and the promise of all those hollow tomorrows now filled with her lovely face. It could even be the New York cop: there was something about his iron, basic integrity that reminded Jason of a simpler world he had once known. It could perhaps be that he was a fighting man, and here was a battle worth his skills, and an enemy worthy of the graveyard. Or perhaps, most of all, it was that the veils of confusion had lifted, and the disturbing grays of right and wrong at last cleared into black and white again.

Where the corridor ended, he could see a patch of light. He knew the layout of ships. There would prob-ably be a square where staircases and passages converged, even upside down. He must go up, he thought, to keep clear of the water. Behind him, he heard Anton gasping as he regained his footing. In his own exhilaration, he almost overran and had to grab a wall pipe to stop himself.

He swung around into the square. It was as he had thought, with one exception. To the left was a staircase. Directly ahead was the round entrance to a duct, and the mesh grill that must have been torn off by people trying to escape. He was immediately aware of both, but they hardly registered on him. For between the two possible exits, motionless and silent, stood the tiger.

It was an awesome sight. It must have been nearly ten foot from tip to tail, and well over three feet high at the shoulder. Its gaudy colors were so strongly marked that it looked like a child's painting.

It studied Jason, still without moving. Then the white tip of its tail twitched, the curving teeth flashed briefly, and it gave a growl. It was a low, moaning sound, a warning, an indication of more to come. Jason's mouth dried and his hands moistened.

He faced the tiger and began to move sideways towards the duct. Inches became miles. First he moved his right foot gently across. Then he brought his left foot up to join it. He moved smoothly, without hurry. He did it again, and again. Another growl from the animal. He was now about four feet away from the duct's yard-wide mouth in the middle of the ship's metal paneling. Jason dived straight into it and felt the relieving cool steel cylinder around him. Hands, knees, and feet all pumped and pulled as he scuttled down the pipe. He didn't feel the times his head cracked on the top or the skin tore on his hands and knees: only the fear that had propelled him down that long barrel just like a bullet.

His light showed him the plain steel of the plated tube and the circle of darkness where it ended. With an effort, he pieced together his splintered thoughts. The tunnel would lead to the central shaft that gave access to all decks on liners of this design. What was in the shaft? Since it ran the depth of the ship, the bottom part must be under water. There would be—there must be—a ladder running the full depth of the ship for the engineers and crew.

He spurted along towards the growing circle of darkness ahead.

Behind him he heard a crash and frantic yelping sounds. Jason spun and pointed the light back up the tube. It was Anton. His gross frame seemed to pack the duct and even at that distance he looked like a misshapen portrait of terror. He too had taken the only possible way out. Then Jason heard the pitiful mewling of Anton fade under a deluge of sound. It rolled and rumbled down the hollow duct, a dreadful, vivid booming that seemed to shake sanity itself. It sank then swelled again, stampeding all reason.

The tiger was coming down after both of them.

The surging tide of noise seemed to bowl Jason along before it. Fast as he went, Anton was catching up with all the power in that vast body.

The end came up like a precipice. Jason did not pause, but only seemed to hesitate as he poised at the mouth, then dived away to his right. In that atom of time, he had seen the service ladder. There was a second of nothingness, when, unanchored, he seemed to whirl in a blackness without space or time. Then his fingers felt the hospitable cold steel of the rungs, and his agitating feet secured on another. His light was still in his hand. He looped one arm through the ladder and shone the light back on the black hole of the cylinder, perhaps two feet away.

If Anton saw him or the glow, he gave no indication. He appeared in the circle and gazed unbelievingly into the gaping depths below him. Then he turned with his legs tucked under him, and the roaring filled the shaft. Jason saw those blinding colors again, the angry snarling face and the paw plucking at the squatting figure in its way.

Anton was smashing profitless punches at the great cat's head. Jason could hardly believe it. He was trying to fight the tiger with his hands. He was pitting his only gift, the unnatural brawn of his body, against the animal. Time after time his heavy fists landed. Twice the beast pulled back its face from the savage pounding.

Then it jumped. In a silence somehow more violent than the tumult of the fight, Jason saw the two figures, the animal and half-animal, drop into the depths locked together. His light could not reach them. He heard only the splash, a last gurgling groan from Anton, and then the pained roaring too finally stopped.

It was only then that Jason realized what he had seen. When Anton had been flung back by the tiger's charge, he had sensed the first primitive fear—the fear of falling. It had even overwhelmed his fear of the tiger. For he had hugged the fearsome beast as he fell to his death.

Moments passed. The cold silence of the wide shaft made Jason shiver. He shook himself. Then he began to climb upwards.

THE PURSE

11

Her relationship with the rest of the group had changed. At first, Hely could not understand why, and she watched in silence, searching for the explanation, as they gathered again in the passageway they called Broadway, and reconstructed the sequence of events.

The nurse again explained to the policeman how she had been the only survivor of the score or more passengers who were led by the doctor towards the ship's bow—the wrong direction. She also examined Martin's foot. "Oh my," she exclaimed, gently testing it. "He must have broken nearly every bone!"

They spoke very little to Hely, and when they did it was always concerning Jason. "Don't worry," Klaas told her. "He's a very capable young man, that one. He'll be back all right." Even Martin, whose interest now seemed centered on the Dutch girl, offered her some consolation. "Anton won't stand a chance with him," he said, cockily. "He'll soon catch up with us."

Coby spoke then, but it was to Martin. "Well, you certainly stood up to Anton, James. No one could have been braver than you. You were wonderful."

Martin blushed, despite the pain. He was still uncomfortable with the memory of how Coby had saved him when Anton had seized his foot. She was obviously not going to mention it. He was grateful. He replied, "I wouldn't have been able to do anything without you." He bit his lips in agony as he tried to pull his sock over his injured foot. He looked up at Hely and said, "Your Jason would sure have been proud of us."

"I'm sure he would," Hely said. She realized now what it was. In the short time they had been together, she had become established as Jason's woman. She was an adjunct to the mysterious American. They were treating her like a wife. She was not sure what her reaction ought to be. In all her life she had never surrendered a scrap of her independence. She had always stood alone. Yet now she was being treated like a woman whose husband is away on a business trip. The thought amused her. She decided she liked it after all.

But how incomplete the group was to her without Jason. They were standing in a close circle in the corridor, their faces shining in the light of two flashes. The policeman looked haggard. His eyes were a tired white against his oily, dirt-caked face, and his clothes were rags. Martin, who had abandoned his sock and shoe now, was balanced on one leg, his arm round

Coby, and he too looked beyond the point of exhaustion. The keenness had been struck from his face by pain. The nurse had now regained her professional composure, but she too was a filthy scarecrow of a figure, her hair hanging in greasy strings. Klaas and Coby were almost elegant in this company, but the strain showed in the father's face as he talked.

"We have been on board something like an hour," Klaas said, glancing at his watch. "I estimate it will take a flotilla of rescue and salvage boats about two hours to get here, and I don't think the *Poseidon* can stay afloat that long."

Rogo ran thick fingers through his matted hair. "I'd like to know how the hell a so-called big-time cruise liner like this can get turned over anyway."

"Perhaps no one will ever know," Klaas replied. "But one thing I can tell you, Mr. Rogo. This is no longer the great liner it once was. The Greek owners are not men of probity. They are little more than gangsters. But that is not our concern. I think we must apply our minds to getting back to the *Magt* as quickly as we can."

"What about Jason?" Hely put the point quickly.

With a shrug, Klaas said, "He is a man who can look after himself. Look, I don't want to leave him here, but there is my daughter to think of. There is Martin. He's badly injured. Anyway, Jason can find his way back as easily as we can."

It was the nurse who spoke next. "I don't know him," she said, "but I don't see how we're helping anyone standing around here."

They were all looking at Rogo. He weighed their words. Then, with a snap of the head, he said, "Yeah, you're right. He's a tough monkey okay. I'm gonna try to get you back up there. But I stay here with the gold. You people can go."

He held the gun out on his open palm. "We only got one gun. If that Bela guy has got any more trained gorillas . . ."

Klaas intervened. "I feel sure he will have many more men. For his sort of salvage work, you would normally have a crew of thirty. Even more."

"Sufferin' Jeezus!" Rogo threw back his head. "If those other guys are anything to go by, the next bunch'll be armed with bazookas. Even if Jason gets back we only got two hand guns."

Martin cut in, "One, Mr. Rogo."

Rogo glared at the one-legged figure. "Two. Jason got one from the guy he bopped."

"That's what I mean," Martin went on. "Anton knocked it right out of his hand. I heard it go into the water."

"For Chrissakes!" Rogo beat the palm of his hand on his forehead. "The stupid bastard! What a helluva time to go lose a gun! I mighta known he'd screw it up. Goddamn freak!"

Klaas noted the policeman's temper with concern. The situation was difficult enough.

"One thing we can do is see if the boiler room is clear," he said. "Then perhaps we can escape from this death trap."

Rogo did not sound very interested. "Okay, Klaas, take my flash and go give a look."

The Dutchman took the light and headed back to Broadway. Rogo watched him go. "That lousy freak!" He was still thinking about Jason and the lost gun. His anger was directed more against their misfortune than Jason himself, but even so Hely felt she must say something.

"You were glad enough of his help," she reminded him. "But for him Bela would have shot you."

He turned his head and gave Hely a look that contained no gratitude. "I coulda made it without him," he said. "Anyway, I still ain't happy about you, lady. That phony line you gave us. What the hell are you doing here? And don't give me more crap."

His eyes had gone cold. He was turning his frustration against her. Hely realized how vulnerable she was without Jason there. She was alone. She looked around the rest of the group. Martin was engrossed in the Dutch girl. Coby had disliked her from the first. The nurse plainly regarded Rogo as the person in command.

"I told you all that," she said. "I explained before. We were looking for survivors."

It sounded weaker than ever. Somehow Hely felt she had lost confidence in her ability to deceive. What had once come to her quite naturally, now seemed unmanageable. She felt exposed and deserted before the policeman's bristling assault. The purse on her belt suddenly began to weigh a ton.

She said weakly, "I don't know why you're picking on me now. You daren't do it if Jason were here."

"Oh no?" Rogo came back. "You kidded him by switching your ass at him. I seen it all a million times. You're a doll. Okay, so the world's full of 'em. My Linda . . ."

He stopped in mid-sentence. The nurse stepped in politely, "Where is your wife, Mr. Rogo? Did she get off the boat all right?"

He turned his paralyzed face toward her. She did

not know. How could she? The nurse rattled along blindly: "My, she really was having a bad time of it with seasickness, wasn't she? I came to see her in your cabin, remember?"

"Yeah, I remember." Rogo's voice was a whisper. "She's dead. She fell. It was . . ." Hours and days had become blurred and it was only with an effort he could work it out. "It was today, I guess. Early today." He slipped his thumb under his suspenders and looked down at those horses. Classy, just like Linda.

The sigh of relief almost whistled from Hely's lips. She could not have resisted the policeman's tenacious questioning much longer. The purse now seemed to have swollen. It seemed to be transparent. She felt sure everyone was staring at it. She must get rid of its contents immediately.

She cast about for a sympathetic face. "What is it you Americans say—I'm just going to the powder room?" Martin nodded. Hely had trilled it with a glistening smile. It rang completely false. She was trying too hard. She walked off as casually as she could down the corridor, knowing that her anxiety showed through the thin flippancy. Martin had not noticed. Rogo was too stunned. But the Dutch girl's quick eyes had been watching and Hely could feel them on her back.

She turned through the first door. It was a store-room. She stepped into the darkness and her frenzied fingers tore at the fastening on the purse. Once she got rid of what was in it she had nothing to fear. Rogo could suspect what he liked, but he could prove nothing. That was all that stood between her and a new life with Jason. She pushed her hand down inside and scooped it around the cold rubber to enclose all the hard richness of her haul. A few hours ago she would have died to defend her bounty: now she was throwing it away. What would Jason have thought if he had ever known?

"What are you doing?"

The question came like a shot. Her heart plummeted. It was the girl Coby. She was watching from the doorway. She spoke again. "What have you got in there?"

No words came. Hely scoured the girl's face for some understanding or sympathy, but found only suspicion and distrust.

The girl called over her shoulder, "Mr. Rogo! She's got something in that funny rubber purse!"

Hely heard Rogo's heavy tread and saw him appear in the doorway. He had sensed the gravity in the atmosphere, for he said quietly, "Okay, Coby, I'll see to this." When he spoke to Hely, the anger was completely gone. He sounded somber.

"Tell us now, lady. We gotta know sometime."

It was all going to be snatched away from her. Her future, transformed by Jason, was to be destroyed by this one wicked hangover from her life before. There was nothing in the world she could say or do that would move this granite-faced man. She dug back into her old life and could find only one hope. She looked Rogo straight in the eyes.

"Leave me alone and I'll do anything."

There was nothing sexual in how she said it. It was not the vamp act with which she had lured the *Komarevo* man into the room. It had none of the sensuality she had often used to beguile men. It was a direct offer, stark and emotionless. It was a trade.

"Anything," she repeated. But she knew from the

open-mouthed shock on his face that he understood perfectly already.

The silent tension snapped as Klaas burst into the room. He noticed nothing, and the words cascaded from him. "Mr. Rogo!" he shouted. "They've gone. I've been up as far as the engine room and it's completely empty. We can go. Let's get off this ship now, before they come back, or before it sinks. It's our last chance!"

Rogo's thumbnail rasped on his unshaven chin. Klaas could not understand why he was hesitating.

"For God's sake, don't you realize?" he babbled on. "I've got a daughter out there. There are women on board. Miss Hely and the nurse. You have a responsibility to get them off, whatever you choose to do yourself."

Rogo made his decision. He quietened the Dutchman with extended palms. "Okay, okay. I get you, Klaas."

He gave Hely a long, significant look. "This ain't over, you know. I gotta sort it out, but not right now. First we gotta get off this tub."

He ushered her out before him, and then roared, "C'mon then, for Chrissakes! Watcha all waiting for? Move it!"

The ragged, limping column began to thread its way back up through the ship. Hely wondered why being honest was so much more difficult than being dishonest. Rogo could have had her. One last time would have made no difference. It was nothing. It was a thing she'd done a million times. Suddenly she wanted to be sick. She did not know what Rogo's answer would have been.

* * *

There was always home to go back to. That had been the one reassurance he had allowed himself throughout the whole nightmare of Vietnam. Jason remembered that quite clearly as he climbed. He went at an even pace up the ladder which scaled the inside of the shaft. Hand over hand, step by step, rung after rung. It was a long way. The silver stripes of the rungs stretched beyond his flashlight's range.

One day, he recalled telling himself, it would all be over and he would be back in the sure and sunlit world he knew. It had been quite exciting at first. He had tried to imagine what it would be like in Vietnam. Truckloads of American soldiers surging into small towns, the streets lined with people, bouquets of flowers, the cheering, the hero's welcome.

And there had been crowds. Crowds of whores and pimps and buyers and sellers and wheeler-dealers, and every smile had a price tag on it. The girls all loved him. By the hour, at the going rate. It was hard to feel like a hero then.

And it was hard too to understand why he was there. It had been so clear before he came. Democracy and freedom, the things he had known in abstract all his life. Patriotism was as simple as baseball. It was different when the black leaves blotted out the wicked blue of the Vietnamese skies, and the silence was itself a conspiracy. Then the unheard whispering among the leaves turned into the mad gossip of gunfire. Then, at his feet, a tiny, twisted body and an anonymous brown face. After that, they fell from the trees like ripe apples, because this was the will of the American people. Then it wasn't the will of the American people anymore. Helicopters dropped from the skies and plucked them off the surface of that suffering land,

and all that remained was the memory of one brown face, the only one that never had a price tag on it.

The rungs felt cold in his hands. He remembered thinking in the helicopter that it was all over. He was going home. Back to normality, back to clean streets; back to old friends and old habits, and the warmth of familiarity would strike the shivers from his bones. But his own father could not lift his eyes. He gripped his hand hard and said something about a terrible mistake. The soothing peace of home became a searing shame. No one would talk about Vietnam. They tried to protect him from his own guilt, and his presence only served to stab their own consciences.

"Hi, where've ya been all this time? Must be two years, nearly. Oh. Gotta be going now. See ya again . . ." They called it Away. "While you were Away . . ." The same word some people use for jail.

So after that Jason flung himself into everyone's battles. In Cyprus, in Lebanon, in Africa. He became an amateur mercenary, a soldier of misfortune, and he took on the grief of the world to assuage his own.

He had been wrong. He was sure of that, as he neared the top of the ladder. But this time at least, he was right. Just for one day the truth was clear. Rogo's rough-hewn integrity must not fall before the unalloyed wickedness of Bela. There was Hely too. Jason had at last found a cause, and a reward.

He saw the entrance to the last duct at the top of the shaft, leaned over and swung himself into it. He was now at the very top of the inverted ship. He began crawling.

"LIKE YOUR PRESENT, ROGO?"

12

For the second time that morning, the smartly painted pinnace from the *Komarevo* came up alongside the jutting remains of the *Poseidon*. This time it was followed by another, and both sat low in the still waters. In each boat there were eight men. Each one carried a Stechkin. Each one was uniformed in maroon sweater and roll-on woolen hat. They looked exactly like what they were: a war party.

Captain Bela regarded them with pride. Their demeanor reflected his own firm belief in discipline and order. This time, he thought, there would be no mistakes.

He checked his watch. It had taken him little more

than half an hour to organize this expedition. A rescue flotilla could not possibly arrive for well over another hour. He had enough men to move the cargo expeditiously, and they were sufficiently well equipped in both arms and experience to cope with any further intrusions. Captain Bela drew on his cigar and, quite consciously allowing himself a little vanity, decided that he had recovered the situation to his satisfaction.

Anton and the other two, he thought, would almost certainly be pursuing Jason and his friends through the ship. Perhaps they had killed them, perhaps not. If they returned by the time the gold had been moved to the *Komarevo*, well and good. If not, then they and any remaining survivors would die when the *Poseidon* finally sank. For sink it definitely would. The grenades on the belt around his waist might help to finish off the stricken ship. It would, after all, be the tidiest of endings to a messy affair. The *Magt* would, of course, be dragged down too, and the world would doubtless be appropriately saddened that a gallant rescue operation should end in such tragedy. But then, thought the captain, the world was easily saddened.

With a flick of slim fingers, he sent the stub of the cigar hissing into the sea. He had never seen a sea so calm, he thought. It was as well. It would make the process of transferring the cargo that much easier and quicker.

He rose in the bow as they tied up to the whale-shaped hulk and reached out for the ragged edge of the entrance they had cut out earlier in the day. He would lead the party on board. He raised himself with a thrust of the foot and felt the sharp edge of steel tear at his finger. "Damn!" he said, and dropped back down into the pinnace. Otherwise, the shot would have hit him between the eyes.

He felt the light sweat cool his face, and held the cut finger to his lips. *It must be Jason.* He thought quickly and without panic. The only guns on board were the ones his men had. Somehow Jason and the others must have disarmed at least one of them. At the very most they could have three pistols, and they were unlikely to present much of an obstacle to his crew.

Quickly he explained the situation to the two boat-loads of men. "Go in commando style," he instructed. "They can only get a sight of you when you are silhouetted against the sky. Roll in fast and they are bound to lose you in the dark. Make your way up into the stern, up under the prop shafts. There's plenty of cover. All the engine-room machinery is smashed up."

Without question or hesitation, the men rose to obey him.

"Did you get him?"

Rogo answered Martin's question with a disappointed shake of the head. "Naw, the bastard ducked just as I was squeezing off the shot. That's one bullet wasted."

They were crouching behind a huge central steam turbine which, when the ship turned over, had been uprooted from its moorings and crashed down between the hold and the now drained shaft that led to the funnel. They had arrived in the empty engine room full of hope, and it was not until Klaas climbed the rope ladder that they saw the two boats packed with *Komarevo* men. The turbine provided the best cover, and, as Rogo had pointed out, it meant they could keep Bela from reaching the gold. Beyond that, there were no plans they could make.

"How many did you say there were, Klaas?" Rogo asked.

"Over a dozen," the Dutchman replied. "As far as I could see they were all heavily armed. With those big automatics, I think."

"Holy Christ!" Rogo said, more to himself than to the others. He looked around at them and once again despaired. A Dutchman who didn't like fighting, a haberdasher on one leg, a nurse, a schoolgirl, and a skin diver who was suspect anyway. His was the only gun, and they were facing over a dozen well-armed, well-trained killers. They might as well take on the entire marine corps!

He was on his knees, peering around the side of the vast metal drum at the square of blue across the width of the ship. Behind them, a little to the right, the hold door stood open, and even in there the brightness of the morning caught the bars of gold. The heavy stench of the tiger was still in the air.

"What kind of a chance have we got?" Martin asked. He was slumped against the turbine, his bared and crushed foot raised on a broken stanchion. His face seemed to have shrunk even smaller with pain and fear, and the terrier eagerness had gone from him.

Rogo was past being considerate. He fell back on the sarcasm that was his customary defense. "Oh, no problem at all, Martin," he said. "Just walk over there and tell that Commie pirate you gotta get back to open the shop and he'll run ya home. What chance?"

Coby's eyes looked as big as dinner plates in her

pretty face. "There must be something we can do, Mr. Rogo."

He looked over his shoulder and said, a little less unkindly, "Don't forget that's American dough in there. They'll be along. We just gotta hope we can hold these sharks off long enough." He lifted the barrel of the gun. "But how long d'ya figure it'll take 'em to realize we only got one gun?"

The nurse began to whimper. Hely, who had said nothing since her confrontation with Rogo, put an arm around her. Klaas consulted his watch. He looked very grave as he said to Rogo, "I cannot see any official rescue flotilla getting here yet. Any passing craft will simply assume that Bela's salvage vessel is handling it."

Rogo's eyes were still on the entrance, his gun cocked. "We might fool 'em for ten, maybe fifteen minutes. After that they're gonna work out our firepower and the show's over, folks."

He looked round at them all again. "I'm sorry," he added, and they nodded mutely. They understood the frustration of his impotence. They understood too that the cop, tough as he was, had been under tremendous strain. He seemed lost without Jason now.

Between gritted teeth, Rogo muttered, "Here they come, the stinking bastards!" The sill of the clean square of blue changed shape for a second as a flattened body rolled over the edge and they heard the bumping and clatter as it landed. Rogo fired, but they knew from his mumbled obscenity that he had missed. He steadied his arm against their metal defense bulwarks ready for the next one. Again the straight black line along the base of the blue square wavered, and again he signaled his failure with an oath.

He turned and dropped onto his haunches among

the others. "Let 'em come," he said, and rested the gun barrel on the floor.

The nurse stifled her sobs and whispered, "Mr. Rogo, please don't give up. You're our only hope."

His face looked aged and sunken as he glanced at her. "I'm just wasting bullets. I can't get a clear shot at them there. We'll just have to let 'em come in and see if we can pick 'em off then."

They could hear the scuffling of the *Komarevo* men swarming aboard. From the noise, it was clear that they were moving into the very end of the stern.

Rogo flinched. A small, sharp object had landed on his head. He picked it up from beside his foot. It was a screw. Then he ducked as he felt another light smack, this time on the ear, and he rubbed the spot and mumbled, "What the hell . . ." and looked upwards.

"Flies annoying you, Batman?"

They all started at the familiar voice, and gazed up. Twenty feet above them, nonchalantly perched on a crosspiece of broken handrail like an owl on a branch, was Jason. He flipped another screw to Rogo, swung down to a lower pipe, and then jumped the rest. He landed squatting at Rogo's feet, grinning at him and said, "I had to come back, Rogo. It's the only game in town."

Hely's face, set and silent before, came alive. She flung her arms round him and buried her beaming smile in his shoulder. Jason sowed a small kiss in her shining hair.

"How in hell's name . . ." Rogo began, but Jason cut him short. "Not now, Rogo. Explanations later, okay? We've got to entertain the visitors." He thumbed towards the stern. "How many are there?"

Grimly, the policeman answered, "Over a dozen.

With Stechkins, and all we have is this pistol and three shots gone already."

He was surprised that Jason did not seem too dismayed by his gloomy outline of their position. All he said was a whispered, "Follow me, everyone," and, ducking down, he shuffled towards the hold, giving a hushed commentary to Rogo behind him.

"Remember my parcels, Rogo? Well, I guess it's a little late for Christmas presents, but I got a little something specially for you. Thought of getting you a thumbscrew or a picture of Adolf Hitler . . ." He was in the back of the hold now, pulling at the smashed packing cases. "But I thought of what old Manny used to say, and got you . . . a surprise."

He turned round and threw something into Rogo's hands. It was a rifle. An old rifle. A World War Two rifle. But it was a rifle.

With a muted whoop of joy, Rogo dived in beside Jason. The case was packed with beautifully oiled and maintained Garand rifles, their polished wooden stocks gleaming, and from another damaged case Jason was prizing ammunition.

They were all crowding round as Rogo passed out the weapons. From outside they heard the gunfire again. It beat out a sinister tattoo all around the engine room. Bela's men were raking the whole place with bullets to try to locate them.

The nurse refused Jason's offer of a weapon. "But I will help with the ammunition," she said. Everyone else was armed, and Jason was shepherding them out of the hold and back behind the safety of the turbine. He talked in urgent whispers all the time.

"You handled one of these, Martin?"

The shopkeeper replied, "Well, they'd been holding

up all the stores around town so I went and took some lessons at the armory. Not with rifles, but the sergeant says I'm quite good if I keep my head . . ."

"Great!" Jason dropped on one knee and leaned to look around the end of the metal barrier. He fired off an experimental shot, then another.

"You okay?" Rogo asked Klaas. Then he saw that the captain was going through the manual of inspection of the professional soldier. He examined all the mechanisms, wiped off some oil, pulled back the firing bolt, and squinted down the barrel. Then he raised himself over the top of the turbine and fired steadily into the darkness.

"Wow!" said Rogo. "Sorry, skipper."

The Dutchman spoke over his shoulder. "All Europeans of my age have handled guns, Mr. Rogo. We had a little problem when I was a young man. Perhaps you heard of it over there in America?"

"Whaddya mean—all Europeans?" Rogo was kneeling beside Jason, and he too was firing. Then he continued the mood of genial whispered jousting. "Who got you outta that mess? I carried one these goddamn things from Omaha Beach to the Rhine."

"Oh, really? I didn't know you'd been an honest man in your youth, Rogo," Jason chipped in. His smile faded when he saw Hely. She was beside Klaas, and she was shooting with the accomplished steadiness of a professional. She saw his look. "Rabbit shooting," she explained, and his grin returned.

Even Martin was joining in, "Hey, Mr. Jason," he said, in a muffled voice. "The address on those packing cases was Mexicana Street, Anaheim. There's no Mexicana Street there I can recall."

"That's right," Jason's reply was low but clear. "And these aren't tins of tomatoes as it said in the manifest." He bobbed around the turbine once more and took a fast shot. "Those Greeks didn't ask too many questions if the money was okay."

"How the hell did you get here anyway?" Rogo asked Jason, between carefully taken shots. Jason explained in staccato sentences. He had climbed the central shaft to the bottom, now the top, of the ship, and made his way through the passages used by the engineers. He knew it was bound to lead into the engine room.

As they crouched down to push in new clips, backs against the steel wall that protected them, Rogo asked, "And what happened to your playmate?"

With mock grief, Jason whispered, "He went out to lunch with the tiger. They died in each other's arms."

The silence from Bela's men was shattered by sustained bursts of automatic fire. It was terrifyingly loud in the metal chamber, and Coby flinched as a wild fusillade combed their end of the room. But no bullets found their way into the sanctuary between the machine and the back of the bulkhead.

Still the only light came through the six-foot square punched out of the side of the boat. Outside, the morning sun was stronger now, and the broad beam which penetrated the engine room half-lit a scene in which the participants could find no point of reference within their experience.

As he had instructed, Bela's men had fled to the far end of the room and taken up positions protected by the jumbled walls of dynamos, rotors, and generators. There they felt themselves to be completely safe, and began to pour burst after burst of gunfire across the room at the huge turbine which sheltered Jason's oddly assorted fighting team.

But they too were shielded by the wrecked machinery, and the *Komarevo* crew waited impatiently for a careless limb to show, or a too curious face to be raised. Their gunfire rattled futilely against the turbine and the bulkhead above them.

In turn, Jason and Rogo and company soon found that they were unable to expose themselves for long enough to return fire. They were locked in a stalemate of safety.

Jason assessed their situation. For all the hideous unfamiliarity of the setting, he realized that what they were fighting was simply a traditional guerilla battle. The battered machinery and the complex patterns of the torn piping, however eerie, were no different from the cliffs and hills and jungles of Vietnam, and victory would go to those who used the terrain intelligently. There must, he thought, be some way to break the stranglehold and turn the pressure on Bela.

Then he had it. He briefed the others in a whisper, and saw small, grim smiles on strained faces.

They knelt in a short straight line beneath the shelter of the turbine, all except the nurse, and lifted their rifles to an angle of forty-five degrees. The precision of their coordination contrasted oddly with their tattered appearance. They looked like some freakish platoon about to fire a military salute.

"Now!" Jason's command set all six guns cracking. Coby fell over backwards from the recoil, but rapidly resumed her position and started firing again. The Garand was too heavy for her to handle easily. Martin had to struggle to keep the angle accurate. They blasted shot after shot into the impenetrable blackness of the top of the hull.

A scream, followed by furious shouting and maddened oaths, came from the far side of the room, and Jason knew his plan had worked. They had concentrated their fire into the curved shell of the hull where he judged it would rain ricochets on their smug enemies, and so it had. Certainly two or three of them had been hit by that random fusillade, and it would uproot them at least temporarily.

Jason and Rogo rose shoulder to shoulder and lifted cautious heads. The *Komarevo* men were too busy scrambling to new positions to be alert now. Rogo caught a glimpse of a white face and quickly made a direct shot. The roar of rage told him he had scored. Jason too began to fire straight across the room into the darkness, and renewed sounds of panic showed he had added to their confusion. The stalemate was broken. Now Bela and his men were the ones under pressure, and they could not reverse the tactic because the bulkhead wall behind Jason offered no helpful angles.

Rogo and Jason talked quietly as they watched, and fired off shots at every moving shadow. It was the talk of comrades, of soldiers of action together, of men sharing the same threat and the same courage.

"Like your present, Rogo?" Jason's grin was reflected in his voice.

"Hell, I like it okay, but Bela ain't so impressed. So this was your little parcel, cowboy? I never took you for a gunrunner." He said it without criticism, but Jason whipped back on the words. "I'm no gunrunner. Well, not what you think of one anyway. That's Bela's trade."

"Okay, okay. Cool it." For once, it was the cop who was soothing the other man. "Where were they going, then?"

"First they were going to some guys I know in Lebanon. That was when the Christians there were having a bad time. Now, I dunno. The Christians suddenly started behaving like lions, and I'm not sure I want to help them anymore. So maybe I'll reroute them to Africa. There are some nice guys down there who are anxious to move along a couple of upstart dictators. Perhaps I can give them a hand."

There was a note of open admiration in Rogo's reply. "Cowboy, you might look like a dopehead but you sure as hell know how to handle a gun. Vietnam?"

"Yep." Jason methodically sent three shots slapping off the side of the hull and grinned at the muffled crashing which followed. "Yep, I kinda got my head screwed up in Nam. Y'know?"

To his surprise, Rogo nodded. "A lotta nice kids did."

They both ducked as sporadic bursts began to come back at them. Bela's crew was obviously regrouping and recovering from the shock reversal.

Rogo rose quickly, fired, then stooped and dropped the empty clip and picked up a new one. The nurse was scurrying from one to another with ammunition. The firing from the other side was building up again, and Martin and the others were shooting mostly in vain now.

"So what's with all this gunrun . . . dealing then?"

"It sounds crazy, I know, but I thought maybe I could help some of the guys the world didn't want to know about. I suppose I appointed myself as world sheriff."

Rogo laughed. "That's one helluva job to take on. Me, I ain't got time to put the world right. Only my corner."

Their faces were barely a foot apart, oil-stained and streaked with sweat, and they exchanged a look of mutual understanding. "Batman, you are so right. From here on out, I just tend my own garden."

"Fine," Rogo answered. "And right now we got this half-assed Commie in our garden. Let's knock the living daylights outta him again."

They were rising when the burst of automatic fire halted, and Bela's clear, pleasant voice came through the darkness. "Talk, Captain Jason."

"You got nothing to say that will interest me, Bela," came Jason's unhesitating reply.

"Perhaps you will correct that opinion when you hear, comrade."

Bela had been thinking. He had been furious at losing the initial advantage in the battle. Two of his men were dead, three more were injured. They had now found new positions among the debris where that hail of ricochet could not reach them. But they were faced with a long fight to try to get rid of Jason and his men and get at the gold, especially now that Jason's group had acquired rifles and ammunition. By the sound alone, it was obvious the guns were not of modern design, but it would still make Bela's job that much more difficult, and that much more protracted. Time was running out.

Then a thought that had been troubling him from the start surfaced from his subconscious. The girl. The skin diver. What was she doing fighting side by side with a policeman of apparently bullheaded integrity, and a romantic idealist like Jason. That was their weakness. He would exploit it.

"I will tell you, Captain Jason. If you should get out of this—and that is very unlikely—how will you account for the fact that your representatives of law and, I believe you call it, order are in the company of a ghoul?"

THE DIVE

13

A mystified silence followed his words. Rogo and Jason made uncomprehending faces at each other. "What's he trying to pull now?" grunted Rogo. Martin, Klaas, Coby, and the nurse all searched each other's eyes for some explanation and found none. Hely was sitting on her haunches. She laid the rifle down beside her. Her face was downcast. The dream was falling apart.

"What the hell's that supposed to mean?" Jason shouted back. He sounded neither interested nor excited.

Bela was relishing every minute of it now. "The underwater lady, Jason. She is the ghoul. She and her friends were robbers of the dead. Thieves, crooks, liars. They had been stripping jewelry off the bodies below. My men killed the rest but she got away. Ask her."

Jason's grin at this preposterous claim hesitated before Rogo's stunned face, and vanished when he turned to Hely. She was as pale as death. She could not lift her eyes to look at him. He could see the glistening lines of tears on her face. He slumped against the cold metal.

Deliberately, very slowly, Rogo rose and walked over to her. His voice was soft and gentle. "We better take a look in that purse now, sister." She did not move or try to hinder him.

His hand scooped down in the bag. For a second he closed his eyes. Then he brought his hand out and opened it for all to see. Even in that dim light the jewels were a handful of dancing lights. And there in the middle of that vision of glittering wealth was the finger, one end a polished nail, the other a ragged, bleeding stump.

Jason raised his head and saw. His whole body tightened. His lips pressed to a thin line, the muscles of his jaw tensed, and the breath came harshly down his nose.

Then he spoke, at first quietly. "I thought you were real. I believed in you." His voice began to rise. "And you were a fake, a phony. A lying, thieving sham. Scum! You are scum!" His fury echoed around her sunken head. "Get out! Go! Get away from me!"

He put his arms flat on the curved top of the turbine, lowered his contorted face, and soundless grief shook his broad back and shoulders.

They were mesmerized with shock. Hely rose, her

face still down, and set off towards the companionway. She moved like a robot. No one attempted to shoot her, or even to speak to her. She seemed suddenly to be in a different world that had no contact with theirs. All their eyes were held by that figure. She was alone in her sin.

By the companionway she stooped and picked up the mask and flippers, the weight belt and air cylinders that were still where she had dropped them when she surfaced in the pool.

Then she did raise her head. In the light from the nearby hole, they saw a face that was a graveyard. It was beyond all guilt and sorrow and pleading and forgiveness. No hope or fear lay in those waxen, still beautiful features.

"For you, Jason, I would have been an angel."

The whispered words seemed to glow in the dark silence. The big American's gripped fists began to beat out a crazy thunder on the steel drum, and he cried again, "Get out! Get out! Get out!" When they looked back, she had gone.

She was walking, neither slowly nor quickly, back down into the ship. The flickering yellow of the boiler-room fires and the smoky grays of the long passage-way passed unnoticed. So too did the distant sound of shooting.

In an odd way, she thought, the jewels in her purse should have been proof of her capacity to love. They proved, surely, that she governed her own body and mind so absolutely that she could become anything or do anything. In the name of so slight a thing as ambition, she had willed herself to be a robber of the dead. In the name of love, what she could have achieved? She could have fashioned herself to Jason's desire. She could have embraced virtue with twice the fervor she gave to vice. But how could she explain that to Jason? He would never have been able to understand.

She came out of her reverie at the sight of the half-open door leading into the hairdressing salon. She looked inside. How could it be that the short time she had spent in that one wrecked room could have changed her life irreversibly? Now all her past had been destroyed. She was marooned in time: no past to return to, no future to advance towards. She had only the emptiness of the present.

Hely stumbled on, passing the theater and the library, until she came to the water's edge, where the sea flapped feebly against the panels of the upturned ship.

Mechanically, she fell into the routine of the expert scuba diver. She spat into her mask to stop it misting, and tugged it on. She heaved her twin cylinders of air onto her back and fastened the straps. She added her weight belt over the other straps in the routine safety procedure. She pulled on her fins. Then she walked into the sea. She followed the darkened water-filled corridors and staircases down into the ship until she found her way to the open sea.

She rose to the surface, lifted her face mask and, treading the water gently, looked around. The *Naiad* was turning to go. She still had time to reach it and leave behind this place of self-revelation and self-destruction.

The glasslike surface was broken by the wreckage that had been shaken from the liner when it crashed over, and the clear horizons only emphasized the hideous carnage that lay all around her. There were crates and bottles, unidentifiable pieces of clothing, an officer's cap, papers, and there, glittering brilliantly not a foot away from her, a plastic Santa Claus. There were shattered spars and a wooden bench from the deck that was now merely driftwood, and an empty lifebelt that must have floated away unused. And yet she felt no urge to return, and for a minute or two she paddled aimlessly and wondered whether to go back to Jason. She could face Bela's bullets or the sullen hostility of Rogo and the others, but she could not face Jason, knowing he would never believe that this Hely was not the one who robbed the dead. She had smashed his dreams as surely as he had smashed hers, and she understood the contortions that had twisted his face.

The water was not blue. If she had not been so self-absorbed she would have noticed it immediately. She looked about again. The sky was clear and cloudless and the January sun bright, but the sea, even in winter a dazzling blue-green, was the color of porridge. Hely was puzzled. She scooped her hand across the surface and examined it. It looked like water taken from a river in full spate. It was murky with particles of dirt. Then she noticed a second thing: it was not cold. At the back of her mind there began to form an obscure and improbable thought. Could it be true? And Jason. What about Jason? There was only one thing to be done. She pulled her face mask down, jackknifed in the water, and kicked off downwards, her uncertainties now dominated by a need for action.

As she swam she saw that the sunlight which

penetrated the surface was drowned by the filth and debris and gallons of oil that congested the water. She could see only three or four meters at the most.

She finned down strongly, her silver hair streaming behind her like a pennant. She checked her depth gauge. Thirty meters. She would have to go much deeper if she were to find out what she suspected. Hely had always guarded her life with care and observed the strict and necessary disciplines the risks demanded. This would be a deep dive. Normally she would not have undertaken it without other divers, without a shot line to guide her back, and without all the apparatus and backup that such a perilous operation required. They no longer applied. This was an act of calculated folly. Her drumming feet drove her on and on. The dirty brown of the surface had turned to the blues of the deep. The water was getting murkier too, and there were none of the unwinking fish that usually come to observe human intruders.

She checked her gauge again. This was madness. She could barely see two meters now. Then, down below her she glimpsed a pinpoint of light. The yard-long fins drove her further, and the light became a glow, a white glow on the ocean bed. All around her, the sea was thick with filth and mud until it was like swimming in a blinding hailstorm, and it was as warm as bathwater.

There was a distant thunder, half-felt, half-heard. The hailstones became pebbles and then rocks, bounding with balletic grace through the water.

The white glow seemed to widen, and Hely saw the whole haunting scene in its light. The bottom of the sea was moving. The earth itself was rising. The underwater cliffs and valleys, normally scenes of silent peace and beauty, were falling apart. One huge ridge of rock lifted, then crashed in slow motion. The light grew bigger. The rumbling became a roar, and the whole floor of the sea swelled up in the shape of a cone, and trembled massively.

Hely could feel herself being dragged down. She had lost her buoyancy by going too deep. She began to sink to the earth shaking below. Hely drove her fins into the water, athletic muscles pumping against the drag. Gradually she began to move upwards.

She glanced at her depth gauge. She had gone far too deep. But if she went up slowly, at no more than eighteen meters a minute, and stopped frequently to decompress, she should be all right. She reached for the plastic card tied to her lifejacket and checked the number of stops she would have to make. Stops of one minute at first, then six minutes, then twelve minutes . . . It was too long. She could not afford the time. There was only one way to get back to Jason now.

With one hand she flicked open the quick-release catch of her canvas belt with its thick lead weights, and watched it sink. Then she opened the tap of her small air cylinder and felt her adjustable-buoyancy lifejacket puff up around her, and she began to rise. She went slowly at first, then faster and faster towards the faint gleam of daylight above, shooting up like a human cork.

She felt giddy and slightly giggly, and recognized with some fear what that meant. What was it divers called it? Rapture of the deep, that was it. The first effects of nitrogen narcosis, when breathing under pressure releases bubbles of nitrogen into the bloodstream. She understood it as well as a doctor can diagnose his own ailments. She had heard too many warnings about the bends not to know what would happen to her.

She focused hard on the task that lay ahead of her. Already she felt strange. It must be the nitrogen putting the brain centers to sleep. She must act now. She must make no mistakes. She tore the mouthpiece away for a moment and began to exhale steadily. That should prevent her from bursting her lungs on that rocketing ride to the top.

She must also retain control of her mind. She conjured up a picture of Jason. She was going to Jason. She must remember that. She glanced down. Her feet were dangling loosely. She was losing the synchronization between mind and body. She concentrated fiercely, and her flailing flippers began again.

She felt weightless, soaring like a bird in the blue. There was no pain. But her arms and legs felt strangely fluffy and useless, and all she could seem to see were the bubbles flowing from her mouth. Silver bubbles, pretty silver bubbles, she thought, shining like jewels . . . The jewels. The jewels and Jason. She must remember Jason. She must hold that one picture in her mind, his grin and those armor-piercing eyes.

There was another thing to remember. Something to help her. All the experts had always told her that the speed with which people succumb to the bends depended on willpower. A strong-minded diver could last much longer than one who panicked. If she thought only of Jason and kept his picture before her then she could do it. She could fight off the waves of clouds that seemed to fill her head. The willpower that had propelled her through life could surely carry her through this one last journey. Then Jason would know that she could have been an angel. Then he would understand. This was the only way she could show him.

The sea was getting lighter now. She had passed all the stages where she should have stopped to decompress. It was too late. The clouds drifted across her mind again. Jason! She tugged herself sharply back with his name. This would prove to him the quality of her love, and that was all that mattered now.

Above her loomed the blurred shape of a ship. It was upside down. She could not think why the ship looked upside down. Of course. It was the *Poseidon*. Jason was in there. The thoughts would not come now, and she had to push them through the thick mist. Dimly she could see that two of the funnels had crumpled and were lying on their sides. The third, the one nearest the stern, was intact. She replaced her mouthpiece, and swam up the side of the funnel. She found the inspection plate. She pulled at the handles. She had seen other handles like that. She remembered: the handles on the hold door, and the tiger, and Jason. She must keep remembering Jason. His face was still there, framed in the clouds. The plate floated off and spun slowly away into the depths, and she slipped inside. She could see pipes. She must follow the pipes. Half pulling herself with her hands, struggling to keep her fins beating the water, she worked her way along. She was in the fiddley, and she knew those twisting tubes that took away the fumes and smoke must lead to the engine room. And to Jason.

Suddenly she was clear of the water. Why couldn't she see properly? There was something in her mask. Her thoughts had got lost too. There was a ladder.

Her fingers were around the ladder. Fingers like the finger she had cut off. Like the finger in her purse that had cost her Jason. He was at the top of the ladder. Swaying and clinging, she climbed rung by painful rung. She saw the fingers come off the rung and felt herself leaning backwards and wondered quite detachedly if they would get hold of the rung again. They did.

Then she was at the top. It was silent. Desperately she fought to push back those clouds again. She began crawling. She saw another picture. This one was the Dutch girl. Hely spoke. She was sure she was speaking, although she heard nothing, and the Dutch girl nodded. Then there was another face, the one she had kept before her all the time she swam, but she did not know if it was the real face or the one she had painted in her mind. His lips were moving but there were no words, and she thought he did know now, he did understand, and nothing mattered after that. Then the clouds swept the skies of her mind, covering everything.

AMONG THE SHADOWS

14

As soon as that black and tragic figure of Hely had gone, Bela dropped back among the shadows of the stern and began whispering instructions. He had gained two advantages with his declaration about the girl. Jason's crew were now one gun short, and it had also given him the opportunity to assess their position more accurately. Now he must act quickly to get at the gold. If only the others had surrendered Rogo, he could have released them and started work on moving the ingots.

Two more of his men began to work their way towards the patch of daylight. They crept on their stomachs through the steel jungle to reach a position where they could pour their fire into the narrow canyon that sheltered their enemies. The rest kept up a steady fusillade.

"Sweet Jesus!" Rogo realized what was happening. From the new angle of their attack, Bela's killers were able to rake the gap at the hold end of their barricade, and that part of their small sanctuary was now loud with the slap and whistle of bullets.

He grabbed Coby's arm and almost flung her up to the end which was still protected. "C'mon, get outta here!" He helped Martin to his feet, and also bustled the nurse away from the danger zone. The attackers could see the gap now and the bullets zinged into the hold, against the door, and ricocheted back against the turbine. They had lost at least half their haven.

"Hey, cowboy." Rogo gently shook Jason's shoulder. He was still slumped against the metal drum. "Jump to it, fella. We gotta have the full team out today." He looked into Jason's face. It was numbed with shock and grief. He shook him again and whispered, "Your old pal Batman needs a hand."

Nothing seemed to touch him. Jason closed his eyes wearily, opened them again, and his voice was a dull croak. "Just when I was beginning to believe again, Rogo. Just when I thought I'd found something that was true. And it wasn't true. She was a fake, like everything else."

Putting both hands on his shoulders, Rogo turned Jason to him. He spoke with surprising tenderness. "I know, pal. I understand. But we still gotta bust these rats."

Martin had dragged himself up to the far end of the barrier and was trying to shoot round it. Coby was with him and gamely firing, although the recoil from the old gun nearly knocked her over each time. Klaas was rising and firing every few seconds, and the nurse knelt behind them, reloading and passing up the guns. Jason took his place alongside Klaas, but he fired automatically and did not speak.

There were barely fifteen feet of their strip of protected territory left, and it was Rogo who stood alone at the end which was slowly opening for Bela's advancing gunmen. It was all Rogo now. He was firing rapidly and talking all the time, and the battle light was in his eyes. He cursed Bela in fluent and blasphemous tones, and then turned to exhort the others. Their morale was built around the plucky cop, and it was only the sight of his undaunted and sweat-streaked face that held up their fading spirits. Jason seemed a blank.

But all the time the angle was opening as the shadows out there moved further around, and gradually Rogo found himself being beaten back. He fired on grimly, his eyes white and wide, and occasionally shot back looks of desperation at Jason, searching for support. The younger American was oblivious to them all.

Soon Bela's men would sneak far enough to be able to pour their fire directly down the channel where they crouched. Then the siege would be over.

There was little to be said. Once, Klaas touched Coby's arm and whispered, "I'm sorry, Coby. I should never have brought you here."

She attempted a gallant smile and reassured him, "It's not your fault, papa. You couldn't have known."

Martin overheard. He too murmured up to her, "You're a very brave young lady, Coby." This time the smile involved no effort. "It isn't so hard with someone like you beside me, James." And the little shopkeeper, drained by pain and exhaustion, felt his limp spirits rise a little.

Rogo had been driven back almost into their midst now. All that was left was a small island. Soon that too would be covered by the withering fire from the Stechkins. He snapped his words over his shoulder as he pumped shot after desperate shot into the dark.

"Listen, you guys. This sonofabitch Bela has got it figured now. Two of his thugs are snaking around under that goddamn hole they cut in the side. Any minute now they're gonna get a clear shot down here. I can't take 'em shooting against the light. So here it is. I'm taking Bela's deal. The rest of you can get outta here, and I'll take my chances with him."

Rogo was trading his life to save theirs. They all knew what he meant, and they did not know how to respond. Klaas glanced at his daughter and thought for a moment, then said, "Well, perhaps . . ." But she cut in, "No, papa, I will not allow it."

Between shots, Rogo's voice came back in a hoarse but insistent whisper. "Look, miss, I'm a cop. This is what we're paid for. We're the guys who catch the flak when you're home in bed. That's the way it is. Christ, I'm lucky I lasted this long in the job. Beat it while you got the chance. He ain't gonna let me leave alive, and what the hell, I ain't walking out on that gold for any goddamn deal."

They saw his streaked and pleading face in the half-light. "Please!"

"No." The one word hit them like a hammer. It was Jason. He was alive again. Rogo's offer of self-sacrifice had penetrated the armor of his stunned apathy, and he took over forcefully.

"Forget it, Rogo. Whatever we do, we don't start

selling out now. Not you, not anyone. And we don't give in that easy either."

The sheer vigor of the man reborn seemed to warm them all again.

"So what do we do?" Rogo's question was not his usual ironic sneer. He was looking for help.

"Okay, I'll tell you. We take out those two guys before they get us." Even as he said it, a spray of bullets rattled behind them against the bulkhead. "When I give you the word, put this light on them, full beam straight in the eyes. I'll jump up there and try to hit them." He pointed to the top of the turbine.

"You'll be dead within seconds," Rogo replied.

"Right," Jason countered. "But it won't take seconds. By the time they've got over the shock of the light and realized I'm up there, I'll be back down. It's worth a whirl."

"Okay." The cop tilted his head questioningly. "One thing, though. You switch the light, I do the blasting."

Jason handed the torch to the reluctant cop and checked his rifle. "Sorry, Rogo. Can't allow that. This is my game. Don't forget, where I been you couldn't walk a hundred yards without some sniper taking a shot at you. I'm trained for it. Anyway, an old guy like you couldn't climb up there without help."

It was settled. Rogo nodded agreement. "But snap it up, Jason. Those Commie creeps ain't no gumballs. They done it all before."

He dropped flat and, wheezing with effort, hauled himself along on his elbows until he reached the end of the steel barrier. He bent his arm around the corner and cocked his head to listen for the position of the men who were firing. He grunted with satisfaction and adjusted the flashlight until he was sure the angle was right. *It has to be right*, he thought. *You don't get a second chance on this one.* He lay quietly listening to the sound of his own heart. It wasn't often that Mike Rogo could hear his own heart.

Jason grasped a pipe that stemmed from the turbine and braced his right foot against it, with his left leg bent, ready for the leap. "Okay," he whispered, and sprang upwards and forward. He landed, caught his balance with a twist of the body, and his gun was at his shoulder as the strong white beam sliced the darkness.

The circle of light enveloped the two men perfectly. One was on his stomach, working his way through a tangle of railings; the other was sitting up pushing a new clip in his gun; both held up their hands to protect themselves from the unexpected, unaccountable glare. The scene, a startling and luminous tableau, caught everyone's attention so completely that it was not until the first shot that they saw the phantom figure, feet apart, standing above them.

The man who was reloading grunted and slumped forward. The crawling man jumped and twitched and then fell back, still and limp. Then the silent seconds were ravaged by blasting gunfire as the automatics roared, and they heard a cry of jubilation ring somewhere from the darkness. Jason swayed, then crashed backwards.

"Oh, Mr. Jason!" The nurse gasped, and snatched his hand to find the pulse.

Instantly he was sitting up. "How d'ya like them apples, Batman?" He grinned, and saw his smile of triumph reflected on all the faces around him.

The nurse tore at his sleeve where a dark stain

was slowly appearing above his elbow. "It's bleeding a lot," she said, "but it's only a flesh wound."

Rogo's hand hauled Jason to his feet. "That was some shooting," he said. "You ever decide to take up crime in New York City, let me know. I'll retire."

"Fine," said Jason. "Now let's go to it."

Time and gold were slipping through his fingers. Captain Bela knelt in the cover of a wrecked dynamo and thought about this delicate equation. They must have been fighting for half an hour now. How many of those beautiful slim bars could his crew have shifted in that time? Enough to make him a rich man for life. He cursed quietly to himself at this day of bungling ineptitude, and searched for a simpler, more direct solution.

First, it was obvious that Anton and the others must have been killed by now. How they could have allowed themselves to be taken by that bunch of raggle-taggle amateurs he could not begin to imagine. But they were gone. Then, just when his plan was about to work, he had again been outwitted. A light and two bullets, and all that time had been wasted. He cursed himself too. It was only a matter of reflexes. If he had recovered from his surprise quickly enough to fire it could have been avoided. And Jason must have lived. There were still two first-class shots operating from behind that barricade: Jason and the policeman. He had lost five men, two more at least were wounded. That did not matter. They were replaceable. What did matter was that he had no choice other than to repeat the operation to smoke out the policeman, and see the golden minutes slide away.

It would not happen again. His Stechkin was trained steadily on the spot where Jason had stood. Two more of his men were working their way back under the light of the square entrance. He cursed them too for their slowness. They were apprehensive now, he knew. Their initial contempt for that ill-assorted band had turned into grudging respect, and they were reluctant to take chances.

He felt no malice against Jason. Bela prided himself on his objectivity. He had always known that Jason was a formidable man, from his reputation alone. He did not profess to understand the motives of someone who would risk his own life to save that of a worthless policeman. But Bela could only find admiration for the man's resourcefulness. He wished him dead only because he stood between him and the gold. At the same time, Bela wished he knew the price of a man like that. Everyone had a price, and Bela would have dearly loved to buy Jason's professionalism. It was a crazy world where two people as skilled as he and Jason were flung into opposite camps like this in the name of obscure political ethics. What couldn't they have achieved together? His pistol hand was unwavering as he held himself ready to kill the man he so respected. What a terrible waste, he thought. Captain Bela hated waste.

He tried once again to imagine the feelings of his adversaries. What would they be thinking? What would they be planning? It must be obvious to them that they could not pull that trick again, that he would be ready for it. They must also know that as soon as their sheltered spot was within range they were finished. They were being worn down. They were outnumbered. They were outgunned. They would have to make a deal with Bela, or die, and he could not understand why they did not do so.

Then he heard noises from behind the barricade. Their firing was only sporadic now. There was a lot of whispering and muttering. He tensed himself for another of Jason's tricks, and cursed again the speeding seconds.

The acrid smell of gunsmoke filled the engine room. The sharp crack of the old rifles sounded steadily among the rapid fire of the Stechkins, and the hollow shell of the stricken *Poseidon* chimed and boomed and clanged as bullet after bullet zigzagged among the tangled steel. It was a place of business —urgent, earnest, lethal business—and the time was past for exhortation and heroic joking.

Bela's men had again insinuated themselves along the side of the hull. They filled the narrow angle of the opening with volley upon volley, and moved still further to widen the angle. Side by side, Jason and Rogo knelt, firing together without pause to try to stand them off. But they were being driven back. With weapons that were over thirty years old, all they could hope to do was delay the advance. They clung to every inch until the last moment of safety had gone.

Klaas came to join them and add his fire to theirs. There was little shooting at the other end now. He leaned against the turbine that had protected them and fired blindly into the black that lay beneath the bright blue of the cutaway section.

"What do you think?" he asked. He scarcely seemed to expect an answer from the two gray, grim faces below him. Rogo flicked up a somber glance. "A can of worms, pal. A whole can of worms," he muttered. There was no need to say it was going Bela's way.

Even Coby knew. She glanced over her shoulder and saw the backs of the three men drawing steadily closer. "They're being driven back, James," she whispered. Martin did not bother to look. He too was quite aware of the desperation of their position. "I sure wish Mr. Rogo's friends would hurry up and get here," he sighed. "Or they're going to be too late."

The *Komarevo* men were concentrating their fire at Jason's end of the bulwarks now, but Coby still strained her eyes to find a target. She could make out the looming shapes of the fallen machines and here and there the light whitened a strip of steel. Then on the floor and only a few yards away she saw a movement among the shadows. It was coming from the hole which drained when the ship lurched. The young Dutch girl swung her rifle to her aching shoulder. Her finger found the trigger and she tried to level the sights on it. Then she saw a flash of silver, and she remembered Hely and the gleaming sheet of her hair. It was Hely. She was crawling towards them. Twice she collapsed face down. Each time she heaved herself up and dragged herself a few more inches.

Coby dropped her rifle and ran to her. She slipped her hands under the sagging figure and pulled her into the shelter of the turbine.

"Look!" she said to Martin. "It's the girl. The skin diver. I think she's dying."

She pulled up Hely's mask, and blood sluiced down her face. Her mouth snatched at the air and her blood-rimmed eyes rolled, wildly off-focus but searching madly for something. Her skin looked translucent.

"What happened?" Coby asked. "Can't you hear me?"

Her lips were moving. Coby bent near that she might feel the panting warmth of Hely's breath on her ear. Words took blurred shapes in the soft puffs of air.

"Yes, yes," Coby said. "I can hear. How deep? How long? Oh no!" She turned to the nurse. "Isn't there anything you can do?" The nurse shook her head.

Then Jason was beside them. He knelt and lifted Hely's head and shoulders limp in his arms. His fingers tenderly touched the soaking silver of her hair and wiped away the blood that crawled down her cheek. She struggled to raise her head and her eyes narrowed as though endeavoring to recognize dim shapes. When her gaze steadied on his face, her head flopped back, and she gave the ghost of a smile.

Her voice was a disembodied whisper. "Now you understand," she said, one soft word at a time. "I could have been your angel."

His bloodstained fingers rested on her cheek. "I know," he said. "I do understand."

Her eyes glazed with conclusive finality. Jason lowered his head, and when he raised it again his lips were scarlet. Coby spoke rapidly. "She swam right down to the bottom, and she says there's a volcano coming up under the ship."

The nurse spoke authoritatively to Jason. "It must have been the bends. Look, she'd thrown away her weight belt and inflated her lifejacket. She must have come up like a rocket."

Jason was puzzled for a second. "You mean, she must have swum back without stopping at all to decompress?"

"That's right," the nurse answered. "Quite deliberately. Every diver knows you must decompress—and what happens if you don't. It was calculated suicide."

A terrible gaunt look settled on Jason's features as he looked at the icy mask in his hands and Coby hardly recognized her own voice as she said, "It was true, Jason. She loved you enough to die for you. She was an angel after all."

"WHO WANTS A DEAD COP?"

15

The scuffling and muttering had stopped. Sensing their advantage, the men from the *Komarevo* stepped up their systematic onslaught in a deafening storm of lead, but the cry of a man's voice sounded loud above it. It was a roar of pain that thinned to a weak groan, and it came from behind the turbine. One of Bela's men cackled in jubilation.

Bela smiled. They were making progress.

"Bela!"

He recognized Jason's voice and answered immediately. "Yes, Captain Jason."

"Can we talk business now?"

"Perhaps." Bela was cautious. Twice the American

had tricked him. On the other hand, one of Jason's men had at least been badly wounded, and Bela was still conscious of his time-and-gold equation.

"The deal," Jason punched out the words. "We leave, you keep the gold."

Bela gave the order to stop shooting and stepped forward into the no-man's-land between the two groups, rapidly thinking of all the possibilities of this new situation. "Why is it suddenly so attractive to you, Jason?"

Again, Jason sounded flatly unemotional. "You got the cop. He was the one who wanted to fight for the gold."

So that was who had shouted. Bela gently rubbed his pistol alongside his jaw. "And what about your famous . . . parcel, I think you called it?"

"The contents are rather shopworn now. They were the rifles we were using."

"Ah." Another mystery unveiled for Bela. But still he hesitated. "And how can I be sure your clumsy policeman is dead?"

"Come and take a look."

Bela toyed with the invitation. "And you shoot me perhaps?"

The reply was on its way before he had finished the sentence. "Come off it, Bela. I'm not you. You know you're safe."

A pleased smile lightened his slim features, and Captain Bela made his way across the room, vaulting the bigger chunks of machinery.

He turned the corner around the bullet-scarred bulk of the turbine, and in one glance took in the pathetic, ragged band of amateurs who had been standing in his way. It hardly seemed possible, he thought. Then he looked down at the figure of the policeman, lying face down.

"He's dead."

Jason nodded. "He's dead, all right. One of your cutthroat bastards got lucky and hit him in the temple."

Bela pushed the toe of his shoe under the slack, heavy figure. It flopped over, the thick arms spread with their palms up. Where the forehead met the receding hair, a gout of blood dribbled a crimson stream into his eye.

"He was dead before he hit the ground." It was a woman talking. She was kneeling beside the body, still holding his wrist. "Poor Mr. Rogo."

Bela had not seen her before. "Who are you?"

She looked up. "I'm the ship's nurse. The last survivor. They found me." Bela saw the torn remains of her once starched uniform and nodded. He was satisfied.

"You can always listen to his heart, you disbelieving bastard," Jason said, but Bela was already stepping back.

"I am alive today because I am a careful man, Jason. But that won't be necessary, thank you."

He looked around and saw another body. It was the skin diver. "So she's dead too, the pretty little grave robber," he said.

Jason's whole body stiffened and he seemed about to move forward when Coby wrapped herself round his arm and answered, "Yes. She came back, but she died soon after." She added weakly, "As you can see."

Again, Bela gave a perfunctory nod. He steepled his fingers and became businesslike. "Very well, I see no reason why you should stay."

"One thing." Jason was relaxed again. "I must take the girl."

Bela shrugged. "And him?" His toe tapped the policeman's bulky figure and he was watching Jason's face.

Jason lifted Hely up easily in his arms and met Bela's gaze full on. "Who wants a dead cop? He was a nice guy, but the fight's over."

"Please." They both turned, in evidently equal surprise. It was the baby-faced man. He was balanced on one leg, his suspended foot bare, like a timid little bird. "Please, he was a friend of mine. We were on vacation together. We sat at the same table and everything, me and Mike."

Boredom and contempt mingled on Bela's face. "I can't imagine anyone wanting that. But take him if that is your wish. Now I must ask you to leave quickly. I have business to complete."

Jason led the evacuation on its tragic trail to Bela's rope ladder. His head was held back and he did not look down at the soft figure in his arms and the long sash of silver hair swinging at his side. Klaas took Rogo under the arms, Martin lifted his legs and, hopping and wincing, followed the Dutchman with the body slung between them. The nurse walked beside them, weeping quietly. Coby backed out last, her rifle trained on Bela right across the room.

Bela was already giving orders to his men to put down their guns and start moving the gold. He viewed the girl with a glint of humor in his eye. "What is this?" he said, with ingenuous surprise. "Don't you trust me?"

"Like I'd trust a mad dog," she called out.

"Ah, so many heroes, *mademoiselle*." Bela sighed

dramatically. "And so many heroines. You should not let your feelings cloud your judgment. It is only business."

He raised his glance to Jason, framed for a moment in the cutaway square. "It has been a pleasure dealing with you, Captain Jason," he shouted. "Perhaps another day?"

Jason's reply was faint. "I should be immensely surprised, Bela. Immensely surprised."

The dapper captain laughed pleasantly as he watched them leave. Coby, still backing out, stumbled for a moment at the bottom of the ladder and then ran up it quickly and vanished over the top.

Bela strode over to the hold and switched on his torch. The slim gold bars were spilling out. He checked his watch and ordered his men to hurry.

Then he folded his arms and hummed an old-fashioned waltz to himself. It had after all been a good day. But then, Captain Bela thought, they would all be good days after this.

The eerie sound of a bosun's whistle wailed in the peace of the Mediterranean morning. It was the Still, the sea's traditional call to attention, and the one piercing note instantly brought the semicircle of survivors to a stiff-backed silence on the after deck of the *Magt*. The oaken-faced seaman who was blowing it removed the pipe from his lips, and Klaas, his solemn voice unwavering, began to read from a small prayer book. "I am the Resurrection and the Light . . ."

This was how it should be, Jason thought. Behind them, sea and sky were the same featureless blue. The mad dash to safety had sustained them all through the first few minutes after they had returned to the

Magt. The ancient engines had rumbled into uncertain life, and the gallant little freighter, shaking from bow to stern, had carved her way furiously through the ocean. Klaas had sensed Jason's anxiety and agreed, and the rapidly organized service reflected the Dutchman's meticulous nature. He produced the battered prayer book and found the correct service. He even found an old hand who still had his bosun's whistle.

He had arranged it discreetly, as Jason stood on the deck and watched the scene of so much tragedy and death, and a few minutes violent happiness, fall behind. At first, Jason could see Bela's men lowering the cases of gold into the pinnaces. Gradually the gap widened as the *Magt* rocked on her way. But now the engines were still. The only sound was Klaas's voice. *Soon,* he thought, *it will be over.*

Four deckhands standing behind the group moved up to the rail and knelt down. They were holding on their shoulders a hatch cover. On it was Hely, sewn into a clean white sheet. Klaas had apologized to Jason: he did not have a French flag on board. The two men at the back prepared to lift the inboard end of the cover, but Jason stepped forward. He looked at Klaas and saw the brief nod of the head, and slipped his arms under that lifeless form as he had when he had carried her off the *Poseidon.* "We therefore commit her body to the deep . . ." The weighted body entered the water with hardly a splash and sank instantly. Klaas continued, the soothing powerful words rolling out, and Jason saw that the waters were smooth again. *She belonged more to the water than to the land,* he thought. He did not want marble crosses and flowers. Now every wave would be a memorial to her. This was indeed how it should be: the healing words and the forgiving sea. ". . . and the love of God and the Fellowship of the Holy Ghost be with us all ever more, Amen."

The bosun's whistle began fluting again, first a high note, then a low note. It was the Carry On. Klaas closed the small book with a snap, the engines shook into life. It was over. Jason was turning to thank Klaas when he heard Coby's cry, "Look! Oh no! Look!" They all rushed to the stern rail.

The *Poseidon* was rising. The spoon-back of the ship was lifting and trembling, like some great, dying beast struggling to stand. The sea around it seemed to boil agitatedly, jets of water spitting from the surface. Suddenly, the *Poseidon* was thrust clear into the air. They watched in silence.

A vast mass of black lava had thrust its way up from the seabed, and the eighty-one-thousand-ton liner lay like a stranded bath toy on top of it. An island was being born. The ancient and terrible forces deep within the earth that had caused the tidal wave were now driving millions of tons of lava up through the water. It was a volcano. The sea boiled and steamed around it, and the air was loud with violent rumblings and sharp cracks.

For long seconds they saw it clearly, despite the steam. Then, in a deafening uproar, the volcano blasted a pillar of flame and smoke high into the heavens. Rocks as big as houses leapt through the air. The sky darkened and the sun itself dimmed, with a rain of ash and cinders as the primeval, imprisoned powers of the earth burst forth.

Explosion followed explosion. The column of white and yellow and orange stabbed at the sky and huge clouds of steam gushed upwards. Then the flames sank back like a guttering firework, and they saw that the top of that priapic mountain was a huge cavern. It gaped open raw and glowing scarlet, like some dreadful wound, and slow streams of coruscating red pumped out and crawled down its black steeps.

The *Poseidon* had gone. It had vanished. Blasted to pieces by the forces of the fire, burned in the heat that melts rocks, sucked into the raging belly of the earth itself. The tragic ship with its ghostly crew of corpses, plunderers, and gold had been totally destroyed.

The air seemed to shimmer with the extravagance of heat and light, and the spellbound spectators on the *Magt* winced before it and shielded their eyes. "It's terrible, terrible," whispered Coby, and she shuddered in her father's arms.

"Like looking into the mouth of hell," Jason murmured.

So mesmerized were they by that spectacle that they did not realize until it was almost upon them. "Look out!" Klaas's warning was only just in time. The twenty-foot-high wave was tearing across the sea. It hit the stern of the *Magt* and fermented madly over the ship's topsides. They felt the decks slam their feet. They were gazing into the foam, then suddenly it was the sky, as the *Magt* pitched and rolled helplessly. For a moment it looked as though the vengeance of the seas that had claimed the *Poseidon* was hounding them too, as wave after wave flung the freighter back and forth. Then the thunderous ocean quieted and they clambered to their feet to look upon a newborn land.

The showering cinders and ash had settled on the water and turned it a dull lead color. The skies had cleared. The eclipsed sun ruled again. The island sat solidly among the waters, crowned by proud clouds of gas and smoke that curled about in windless air. The sea hissed around its base and the bloodlike streams slithered down its heights. But the tumult of birth was over. There was no trace of the *Komarevo*. She too had been committed to the deep.

The beer splashed noisily in the tin mug as Jason tipped it out of the can. "Ladies and gentlemen," he said, smiling at the small group around the wardroom table, "I think this occasion calls for a toast, and here it is. To the liveliest corpse in the world!"

The odd assortment of mugs and cups and glasses clinked amidst the laughter. Mike Rogo acknowledged the tribute to him with a mock scowl that would have frightened a grizzly bear. "I don't see what's so goddamn funny." Then he too burst into a growling laugh, and killed a glass of beer at one swill. "Let's hear it again, Jason," he called. "My bosses are gonna wanta know what happened while I was asleep down there."

Jason sat and locked his fingers on the table. They were all free now of the terrible strain. They were rested, washed, and changed into a variety of sweaters and trousers that Klaas had produced. The empty plates on the table were the only remains of a magnificent soup Coby had made, and now they were relaxing. The pale lamp burned dark yellow above them, and the aged furniture gleamed. They luxuriated in the warmth which came of the release from unendurable tension.

"Just like you, Rogo, to sleep through the last act." He had teased the New York cop relentlessly about the way he had been carried off the *Poseidon*, but Rogo was taking it well.

"Okay, here it is," Jason went on. "It was all straightforward. I bopped you on the button, smeared the blood from my arm on your head, and the nurse pronounced you officially dead."

Rogo tentatively massaged a bluish bruise on his jaw. "You punch your weight and then some, pal," he said. "But howdya sell a pass like that to Bela?"

Giggling slightly, Coby joined in. "It was so funny. Well, it seems funny now. Jason said 'No one wants a dead cop,' and pretended he was going to leave you."

Jason continued, "That was the bit you really would have liked. Our Mr. Martin here ought to get an Oscar. He did the scream for you when you were supposed to be shot. Hell, he nearly frightened me to death with it. Then what was it you said to Bela, Martin?"

James Martin had his injured foot, now cleanly bandaged, resting on a chair. He was still pale, but he looked lively enough as he struggled to keep his chin above one of Klaas's big sweaters. "Well, I just said that you were my friend and, and . . ." He paused to check the cop's face. ". . . me and Mike were on vacation together." He paused, then added, "Mr. Rogo."

"That's better. Let's have a bit of respect round here," said Rogo, failing to hold off his own grin. "So everyone gets to take the mick out of me and all I get is a busted jaw. Hey, Jason, you're supposed to be the brains of this outfit. Why didn't you think of telling me the truth?"

"Telling you, Rogo? Are you serious? In the first place, you wouldn't have left your precious gold for anyone or anything. And in the second place you wouldn't have believed a story like that. Not from . . . not from Hely anyway."

For a moment, silence descended on the group and the cheerful banter subsided. They were thinking of the extraordinary woman who had died to save them.

"Okay, you bunch of bums." Rogo was rising, and he lifted his refilled glass above their heads. "Now I wanna make a toast, and this one's serious. Let's drink to the bravest lady we're ever gonna know. And she was a lady." They came to their feet and drank.

When they sat down again, the talk warmed up and Coby used the noise to shield her words to Jason. She touched his hand on the table. "I only pray that one day someone will love me as much as she loved you," she whispered.

He squeezed her hand. "An awful lot of fellas are going to love a girl as pretty as you, Coby," he said, and a blush the color of wine burst over her face.

The desperate air of loss and incompleteness that had haunted Jason when they first returned to the *Magt* had gone with the committal and the sinking of the *Poseidon*. He glanced up at the nurse's question to Martin: "What are you going to do now, Mr. Martin—after you've had your foot looked at, I mean?"

"Join the marines, I guess, Martin, huh?" Rogo chipped in.

Martin wriggled with pleased embarrassment. "Not really, Mr. Rogo. I think I've had all the excitement I can stand. I guess I'll just go back to pushing argyles across the counter in Anaheim. And you, Mr. Rogo?"

"Me!" said the cop, and he slumped back and stretched his legs. "It ain't what I'll do, it's what I won't do. And I'll tell you what that is. Nobody better ever try to get me on a goddamn boat again—not even for a row around the park. These feet won't leave land for nobody. But Jason's the guy whose plans I wanna hear. What about it, cowboy?"

Jason lifted his eyes to the ceiling. "I have decided that I don't believe in the perfectibility of the world anymore..."

"Jesus!" Rogo interjected. "He's lost me already."

"Listen now, Rogo, I'm trying to educate you," Jason said, joking. Then he was serious again. "No, I've decided that the sins of the world aren't necessarily all my fault. I think I'll focus my mind on trying to be an average, decent, knockabout fella. That's about as far as my ambitions go right now."

"Hey, did ya hear that?" Rogo said. "Robin Hood walked out on the job."

The door of the warm room flung open and Klaas came in on a breeze of cold air. He slammed the door behind him and waved a piece of paper in the air. "More messages," he said. He looked specifically at Rogo. "The American embassy has arranged for one of their representatives to meet Mr. Rogo and the entire party, and we are not to speak to anyone at all until we have seen him. They stress that it is vitally important."

Rogo sniffed. "Sure they do. Their representative. I like that! It'll be one of those goddamn kids with shades and a black belt in judo—the CIA monkeys. 'Fraid we'll all gonna be buttoned up tight."

Martin nodded. "It's only natural, I suppose. They won't want anyone talking about what really happened on the *Poseidon*, will they?"

"You bet they won't," replied the policeman.

"And, Jason." Klaas had a twinkle in his eye as he addressed him. "We shall be in Athens very soon now. I thought perhaps you would be planning to leave our company, excellent though it is."

With a laugh, the young American rose and clapped Klaas on the back. "You might just have something there, you old rascal. I guess I'd better slip away into the night, as they say. Hell, if I land in Athens someone might ask to see my driver's license. It'll cut the complications if I just vanish."

"Talking of complications," Rogo said, "I got two big ones bugging me. First, that goddamn lady's gun they gave me. It went down with the ship."

"Is that worth worrying about?" asked the nurse.

"It sure is," he insisted, and looked around the group for sympathy. "When I get back I gotta fill in about a thousand lousy forms to explain it. Those goddamn pen-pushers in the police department'll make a month's work out of that."

They all laughed at his aggrieved apprehension.

"And the second one?" Martin asked.

"The second one is that nobody's gonna believe I tried to sit on that gold. I can't even prove it was there. What kind of a dumb cop does that make me?"

The Dutch father and daughter exchanged sly glances. "I think it's time for your little presentation, Coby," said Klaas.

She reached under the table and tugged at a drawer. Her impish grin flickered in the lamplight and she adopted a formal tone. "On behalf of all those who had to put up with your naughty language and bad temper, it gives me great pleasure to present you with this!"

And she banged her hand down on the table and removed it to reveal a bar of gold. Silence reigned.

Against the dark of the mahogany, it seemed to glow with a light of its own.

"Sweet suffering Jesus!" Rogo could say no more for a whole minute. Coby grinned delightedly at his stupefied reaction. Then he asked, "How the hell did ya get that out?"

She rushed through the explanation. "It was lying on a steel plate near the rope ladder. I've no idea what it was doing there. But that horrible Bela was being all clever and I thought I'd take it for you. I told papa and he thought your government might like a teeny bit of their money back."

"Well, I'll be . . ." Rogo's astonished face looked all around the room and then broke into a huge grin. "That's one helluva souvenir to take back!"

It was little James Martin who capped the whole conversation. His face set rigidly, he leaned across the table and tapped the policeman's hand. "Sorry we forgot the tigerskin rug." Rogo's great gale of laughter swelled as the others joined in, and the sound echoed across the silent seas outside.

The moon was as cold and clear as steel against the black velvet of the night sky. The chugging engines pushed the *Magt* determinedly toward land, and the sea, which had lost its unnatural calm, slapped reassuringly against the bow. Jason was packing his equipment into the rubber dinghy on the deck when he saw the shadow beside him.

"Hi there, Rogo. Taking the air?"

"Yep. Before those CIA vultures sink their claws in." He leaned back against the rail on his elbows and watched Jason neatly stowing everything away. "What're you really going to do now, Jason?"

The young man continued working as he talked. "Well, I thought maybe I'd start a sailing school. Back in the States. I kinda like playing around with boats. It's about the only damn thing I'm any good at. But I lost my yacht in the storm so I don't know how the hell I'll raise the money. Still, I'll worry about that later."

Rogo grunted. They were silent for a little while, easy in each other's company.

Then Jason walked over and grasped the rail with both hands and leaned on stiffened arms. His eyes were fixed on the sea where the moonlight scattered on the ripples, and he spoke in a low voice.

"Tell me something, Rogo. You're a cop. You've seen a lot. Tell me about Hely. How could she be so bad and so good at the same time? I don't understand."

Rogo folded his arms on his heavy chest and thought for a moment before replying. "Y'know my wife died on that tub? Linda. She was . . . hell, she was my whole goddamn life. I worshiped the kid. Know how I met her? She was a hooker. A hooker, Jason. But she was one helluva great broad."

He was almost talking to himself now. "Me? Yeah, I'm a cop. I could just as easy've been a hood. Where I grew up you did your talking with yer fists. I got lucky. I got pulled into a boxing club. From there I got to be a cop. Which side of the law you land on is chance. You got a nice daddy and a swell house and proper schooling"—he brushed away Jason's unspoken protest with one hand—"so you don't know what it's like on the tough side of town. Survival, that's what it's all about.

"Hely. I didn't know the kid. But I know how it

happens. Mebbe she didn't have the breaks you had. Mebbe she had to grab all her life, like Linda did. I enforce the law, right? But I know that the law looks fine for guys like you in the big houses. It don't look so sacred when your belly's empty.

"I gotta tell you this, pal. It takes guts. It takes guts to go against the rest of the world. It takes guts to pull a gun or rob a bank. Don't forget, it was her guts saved us all in the end."

He stopped. He was thinking about Hely's unexpected offer to him when he had tried to search her purse the first time. She had offered herself, and he knew it. "Take it from me, Jason, that broad would have done anything for you. Most people don't get that in a lifetime. You had it for a coupla hours. Call yourself lucky."

They were quiet for a long time then, each one thinking about the woman he had lost. Finally, Jason turned to the policeman and said, "Thanks, Mike. I wanted to believe in her. You just showed me how."

A PRESENTABLE STORY

16

The young man who said he represented the American government, without actually specifying any particular department, had a college-smoothed accent, a permanent suntan, and a worried look on his face. His instructions had been explicit and urgent, and so far everything had gone to plan. The second the *Magt* had docked in Athens he was on board, together with officials from the Dutch embassy and the Greek government.

There had been a lot of talk about security. National security, NATO security. There had been a lot of talk about international incidents and leakages. Martin and the nurse had eagerly given him their assurances and, prodded by the Dutch official, Klaas and his daughter had done the same. He was perfectly satisfied with their response, and with the enthusiasm with which they agreed on a presentable story for the world.

It was the New York cop who worried him. It had been plain from the start that Rogo disliked him, and he made little effort to conceal the fact. He grumbled about "CIA monkeys" and he wore an air of surly truculence that was not at all promising. And now here he was at the inevitable Press Conference, and the young man was not at all sure that Rogo would carry it off. He was not at all sure that Rogo considered it worth trying to carry it off. And it was Rogo, sitting in the center of the group behind a gleaming mahogany table, who would face most of the questions.

Under the white glare of the television lamps, the story unfolded slowly before the prompting of seventy or more journalists. Rogo had been on an assignment to deliver files of documents from the American government to Athens. No, they were not vital documents. Just sufficiently important to require routine security. No, he had no idea of the contents. The papers were stashed in a small hold off the engine room. He had left the ship when it seemed certain the *Poseidon* was sinking. He returned when he learned it could in fact float for hours. Oh yes, and he regretted pulling a gun on the French helicopter pilot. It was the only way at the time. Yes, he had retrieved the documents and they had been safely delivered.

Then it was Klaas's turn. He had gone to the distressed liner and boarded her to see if there were any survivors who required help. The other ship, he explained, was the *Komarevo*, a salvage vessel under the command of a Captain Bela. He had insisted on staying on board the *Poseidon* in order to claim salvage rights. Yes, he agreed, it was a tragic miscalculation. The other boat on the scene, he said, was a pleasure yacht that was merely indulging in some ghoulish sight-seeing.

One by one the questions were tidily answered. The young man's frown was clearing. It was all going beautifully. Rogo explained about Manny Rosen. The poor man had been flung into the water when the ship lurched, and had drowned. Martin had also injured his foot under falling machinery. Martin delightedly put his cleanly bandaged foot on the table for the photographers and said it was nothing really. Then he ran into trouble: Why had he returned with Lieutenant Rogo? He stumbled. "Well, I dunno . . . I guess . . . Well, we sat at the same table." There was an incredulous silence.

"You went back because you shared the same table?" The young man's fingers locked tightly on his knee.

Rogo took up the question. He leaned forward and fixed the reporter with his best, open-eyed, move-along stare, and said, "I asked Rosen and Martin to help me. It was a tough spot. I couldn't call a patrol car. He came 'cause he's got guts and he's too modest to say so. Okay?" It was sufficient. Rogo's authority and the offer of a romantic angle was quite enough to satisfy them.

The young man relaxed and revised his opinion about New York policemen.

They romped through the rest of the questions. "Lieutenant, what's the first thing you're gonna do when you get back home?"

"Check up on what you guys write," came the answer, and a murmur of amusement greeted the typical tough talk.

"What if they call you a hero?"

Rogo shook his head. "The only hero," he said, "is the guy who's been standing in for me back home."

The lights dimmed, and soon they were all shuffling out, sticking pencils and notebooks in pockets. "Lieutenant, I want to thank you," the young man said. "You should be on Broadway."

"I am," said Rogo, with one of his more ferocious scowls. "Only I don't get my name in lights. And can I give you a tip, fella? A word of advice from an old dumb cop? Don't wear those goddamn shades—a kid of ten would know what you're about."

Under the dark glasses, the cheeks pinkened.

Then one of the reporters called out a last-minute question. "Hey, lieutenant, one more thing please. On the television footage there was one shot where it looked like there was a guy in blue jeans with you. Was that right? And if so who was he?"

They were all looking at Rogo. He appeared to be fascinated by the question. "A guy in blue jeans. Hell, I wouldn't know about that. Maybe it was Batman." The roar of laughter ended the questioning and they all trooped out.

In the street, one reporter caught another's arm. "Hey, just a minute," he said. "What was the name of that little guy with the smashed foot?"

"Martin," came the reply. "I think it was John Martin."

Inside, Rogo drummed thick fingers on the table and grinned at his own joke. Hell, Jason would have loved that. Perhaps he'd see it in a newspaper some-where.

He got up and strolled over to the window. Funny guy, he thought. Kinda grew on you. He wondered where he was now. He remembered the final scene when they had parted. They had all gone up on deck to say good-bye, and as they shivered in the night's cold it seemed strange to be separating after the con-centrated intimacy of their few hours on the *Poseidon*. Somehow it had become a solemn moment. The handshakes, the "Take care" and "Watch yourself, pal." Coby's tears when he kissed her cheek. Then that private moment when his eyes met Rogo's and he said, "I never thought I'd take advice from a dumb cop, but thanks all the same, Rogo." He had just mumbled a few embarrassed words himself. His moment had come when Jason was about to pull at the oars. Rogo relished the memory of that again.

"Hey, Jason," he had called. "Check your sandwich can."

He saw Jason's questioning glance as he reached for the can Coby had packed with food. The lid came off and the bright moonlight shivered on that shining ingot.

Jason whistled. "I thought your government wanted its gold back?"

"What gold? It all sank. Remember? Buy yourself a new boat, huh?"

Then his shape had merged with the shifting shadows of the sea and they could only hear his reply, "Okay. And I'll call it the Dumb Cop."

Their laughter met and merged over the water. Then it was silent again. That, thought Rogo, was one helluva way to start a New Year.

* * *

There is a point where the politics of business and the business of politics blur and fuse. There is a time, too, when boardroom faces begin to look the same. Their words, in Greek or English, ring with the clear innocence of simple trade, but, like ocean liners, they may carry a deadly, unseen cargo.

So it could have been Haven or Stasiris who presented a shiningly benign face to his now untousled, unruffled audience.

"Gentlemen," said Stasiris, or perhaps Haven, "I have the pleasure to report that the operation has been brought to an entirely satisfactory conclusion."

Relief relaxed their shoulders, took the tension out of their necks, and unlocked tightly clasped fingers. The sigh was almost orgasmic.

"The facts," continued the Greek or American, "are these. The seismographic station on Malta reports that an underwater volcano which must have caused the original tidal wave erupted this morning and blew the *Poseidon* to pieces. There is now a new island in the sea where the liner lay."

He paused to savor the pleasure of that moment. Then Stasiris added, "You will share with me a sense of sadness that the gallant Captain Bela, who was in charge of the operation on our behalf, died in that explosion. So, too, regrettably, did all his crew."

He paused again. "However, we must balance that against our pleasure that Michael Rogo, the policeman, and other survivors have been saved . . ." He held up a firm hand to silence the first murmurs of doubts. "And, my friends, he was met in Athens by a representative of the American government who impressed upon him the need for discretion in this matter.

"He cooperated, of course, as any good policeman would. The world's press has been given an acceptable account of the incident which will cause embarrassment to no one. Turkey will not have any reason to be offended. Our Greek Cypriot friends might have to wait a little longer. If the American government wishes to repeat the attempt to help an ally with some form of loan, they will no doubt exercise greater caution in the future."

A delighted hum erupted from the smiling faces around the table greeting his last words.

"And, most important of all, the cargo was completely destroyed. Not one bar . . . I apologize, gentlemen. Not one item of the shipment survived the blast."

It was worth saying again. "Not one."